Sara Looked At His Face,

gentle in sleep, and thought, this is how he looked in the past.

Now he was a dangerous, tormented man, desperately in need of help, yet bristling defensively at anyone who came too near his pain.

But Sara understood him. The floodgates had opened, and a tide of desire had come sweeping through and engulfed her. She could make him hers; she saw that in his eyes. All she needed was the chance.

He'd chosen this dangerous path because there was nothing in the world he feared to lose. Sara knew she had to make him love and want her so desperately that he'd refuse to do the thing that might separate them. She had to make the past release him. It was as simple—and as difficult—as that.

D0456474

Dear Reader:

Series and Spin-offs! Connecting characters and intriguing interconnections to make your head whirl.

In Joan Hohl's successful trilogy for Silhouette Desire—*Texas Gold* (7/86), *California Copper* (10/86), *Nevada Silver* (1/87)—Joan created a cast of characters that just wouldn't quit. You figure out how *Lady Ice* (5/87) connects. And in August, "J.B." demanded his own story—*One Tough Hombre*. In *Falcon's Flight*, coming in November, you'll learn *all* about . . .?

Annette Broadrick's *Return to Yesterday* (6/87) introduced Adam St. Clair. This August *Adam's Story* tells about the woman who saves his life—and teaches him a thing or two about love!

The six Branigan brothers appeared in Leslie Davis Guccione's *Bittersweet Harvest* (10/86) and *Still Waters* (5/87). September brings *Something in Common*, where the eldest of the strapping Irishmen finds love in unexpected places.

Midnight Rambler by Linda Barlow is in October—a special Halloween surprise, and totally unconnected to anything.

Keep an eye out for other Silhouette Desire favorites—Diana Palmer, Dixie Browning, Ann Major and Elizabeth Lowell, to name a few. You never know when secondary characters will insist on their own story. . . .

All the best,

Isabel Swift
Senior Editor & Editorial Coordinator
Silhouette Books

LUCY GORDON
Eagle's Prey

Silhouette Desire

Published by Silhouette Books New York

America's Publisher of Contemporary Romance

SILHOUETTE BOOKS
300 East 42nd St., New York, N.Y. 10017

Copyright © 1987 by Lucy Gordon

ISBN: 0-373-05380-0

First Silhouette Books printing October 1987

America's Publisher of Contemporary Romance

Printed in the U.S.A.

LUCY GORDON

is English but is married to a Venetian. They met in Venice, fell in love the first evening and got engaged two days later. After fifteen years they're still happily married. For twelve years Lucy was a writer on an English women's magazine. She interviewed many of the world's most interesting men, including Warren Beatty, Richard Chamberlain, Roger Moore, Sir Alec Guinness and Sir John Gielgud. She also has camped out with lions in Africa and has had many other unusual experiences that often provide the backgrounds to her books.

One

Sara Tancred studied herself in the large gilt mirror on the bedroom wall, her eyes gleaming with satisfaction. Her ash-blond, shoulder-length hair fell in soft waves about her perfectly made-up face. The dark blue of her eyes had been subtly emphasized, as had the soft fullness of her mouth.

The contours of her slim figure—high breasted and tiny waisted—were accentuated by the long, black dress. An unexpected situation had cropped up and the gown's discreet seductiveness and elegant simplicity would be ideal for her purpose.

"Full war paint," Sara murmured to her own reflection. "Let's hope Fergus Drummond is very susceptible, because I don't have much time."

Liz Kellan, her hostess, looked into the bedroom. She was a good-natured young woman of about thirty, whose indolent manner masked a calculating intelligence. Her hobby was spending her husband's vast fortune, mostly on lavish parties in their London home, with guests chosen from the rich and famous.

Sara Tancred was something of a "catch" for Liz. At twenty-seven she was on the way to becoming a celebrity, and her particular skills were fast accumulating her a tidy sum.

"Fergus is here," Liz said, coming to stand by Sara and studying her. "You look marvelous. He'll be knocked out."

"He hasn't brought any female company, has he?" Sara asked.

"No, don't worry. You'll have a clear field," Liz assured her. "I wish you'd tell me what you're up to, Sara. One minute you were enjoying the party like any normal guest. Then I happened to mention that Fergus Drummond was coming, and you dashed off to touch up your make-up, which was already perfect. What's going on, Sara?"

"There isn't time to go into it. If I'd known he was going to be here I'd have filled you in. You might have been able to tell me a few useful things about him at the same time."

"Well, I suppose you know about the trial?"

"No, what trial?" demanded Sara.

"Liz, are you going to spend all evening up here?" The door had been flung open and Liz's husband, George, stood on the threshold, obviously annoyed. "You've got a crowd of guests down there. Save your gossip for some other time." With that he stamped out as suddenly as he'd arrived.

"You know," Liz said carefully, "if my husband wasn't worth several millions, one might be tempted to mistake him for a charmless lout. Look, I'll tell you quickly—"

"Never mind." Sara knew how ill-tempered George could be. "Whatever the trial was about, it can't affect what I'm after."

"You look like someone who's hunting big game."

"The biggest," Sara confirmed with a mischievous look. "But I'll have to play it by ear. Sometimes you get the best results that way."

Together they went downstairs to rejoin the party. Sara was glad Liz could point out Fergus Drummond, otherwise she might never have noticed him. He seemed to be in his early forties. He was above medium height, neither very fat nor very thin, with mousy hair and features that were pleasant but unremarkable, except for a slight crookedness in his nose. His sharp blue eyes held a watchful, hard expression. Despite his mediocre appearance he was one of the wealthiest industrialists in England, and he was the "big game" Sara was hunting tonight.

Holding a glass of tonic water, she eased her way forward until she was standing just by his elbow. Fergus was absorbed in his conversation and didn't see her. As soon as he made a slight movement in her direction she nudged him, spilling her drink with a startled cry. "Oh hell, I'm sorry!" he exclaimed, turning. His voice held a faint burr that proclaimed his Scottish origins.

"I expect it was my fault," Sara said, looking up at him with shining eyes. "I was so fascinated by your discussion that I must have bumped against you."

Fergus's gaze was riveted on her, and Sara felt a small flutter of nerves. It was just possible that he'd seen the recent magazine article that described her as "a woman who'd go anywhere and do anything." If so, he'd be on his guard and carrying out her plan would be more difficult. But she'd have to chance that.

"Look," Fergus said at last, "why don't we get you another drink, then we can introduce ourselves. Have you had dinner?"

As they walked away together Sara gave an inward sigh of relief that Fergus had fallen for it. He'd seen only what she'd meant him to see, the slim, curved figure, the admiring smile. He hadn't noticed the decisive tilt to her chin or the confident glow in her eyes. It was the look of a woman who'd learned that she could always get what she wanted, and was set on getting it this time, too. From now on everything would be easy.

Sara waited until they were seated in a dark corner of the expensive restaurant and Fergus was pouring the wine before she said, "Mr. Drummond, I have a confession to make."

He grinned. "The name's Fergus, and I didn't really knock your drink over you, did I?"

"No. I spilled it myself to get your attention. I had to talk to you. I want you to let me go to Farraway."

"Farraway?" The amusement faded from his face.

"That little island of yours off the coast of Scotland. Fergus, I'm a wildlife photographer. I'm doing a book about rare birds, and I want some pictures of the golden eagle. I've been told there's a pair that nests on Farraway, and I'd like your permission to camp there for a few days."

He was regarding her with fascination. "And this is the only reason you sought me out? You cunning little schemer! Sara, you're an extremely clever and determined lady. I respect that, and although I have to say no, I'm going to explain why so that you don't think I've just dismissed you without thought on the subject.

"Farraway is a special place for me, because of my sister, Laurel. We were very close, and we both loved the island. When our father died he left it to her, and then to me, if she died childless."

"She's dead, then? I'm so sorry."

"Yes, she's dead. She was murdered by her husband, eighteen months ago," Fergus declared heavily. "Rorke Calvin is as vicious and evil a man as ever lived. The poor little soul adored him—God knows why!—but all he ever wanted was her money. He actually killed her on Farraway."

Sara was appalled. "I . . . I am sorry," she said hesitantly. "I hope he was caught and punished."

"I'm afraid not. He was arrested but, he's walking free at this moment."

"You mean he was found innocent? How can you be so sure he did it?"

"Because I saw him. And he wasn't found innocent. We have three verdicts in Scotland: Guilty, Not Guilty and Not Proven. The case against Rorke Calvin was declared Not Proven."

"But if you actually saw him do it—"

"I did. I saw him throw her from the top of a cliff. He claimed it was suicide and he was trying to stop her, but I saw what really happened. She was struggling in his arms, and I heard her pleading with him not to kill her, but I couldn't reach them in time.

"Unluckily I was the only witness and it was a dark night. His lawyer managed to suggest just enough doubt to get the verdict reduced to Not Proven. Rorke Calvin walked from the court a free man, and he had the sense to vanish immediately afterward. He knew what would've happened if I'd gotten anywhere near him."

"I feel awful," Sara said wretchedly. "I had no idea. My publisher only decided at the last minute that he wanted golden eagles, so I had to do everything in a rush. I heard there were some on Farraway, and I called the Highlands and Islands Board to see who owned it. They gave me your name, but of course they didn't tell me anything else.

"I left a message with your secretary this afternoon, but you were out. Then I went to the party tonight, and you were there. Oh Fergus, I feel awful."

Fergus laughed good-naturedly. "There's no need for you to feel badly, but now you know why the island is private." He hesitated. "Look, tell me what you had in mind. Where were you planning to live?"

"In a tent, near the eagles."

"No, that's out of the question. It's wild and windy up there, and Farraway's completely uninhabited now."

"But I'm used to those sorts of conditions," Sara said eagerly. "I've lived in tents and caves all over the world." She could have said more, but although she liked Fergus she couldn't have confided to him her mysterious joy in solitude.

"I'm sure you're very hardy but—" Fergus broke off, and sat brooding for a few minutes. "If I let you go, you'd have to live in the house," he said at last.

"You mean, you agree?"

"I think Laurel would have wanted me to. She loved the eagles." He sat, lost in thought. "There's another condition," he said at last. "You'd have to call me from the mainland after a few days to let me know you're safe.''

"Of course."

"When would you want to start?"

"At once. I don't have much time."

"In that case, why don't we finish our meal and I'll take you home to pick up the key to the house?"

As he drove her toward his house he said, "Don't you have a boyfriend who objects to your traveling to all these wild places alone?"

"If I did have a boyfriend I wouldn't let him tell me what to do," she said, laughing. "But I'm a reject at the moment."

He grinned. "Now that's something I don't believe."

"No, it's the truth," she said lightly. "The last man in my life went off and married someone else."

That was six months ago and the pain had faded now. What hadn't faded was an indefinable unease. Sara knew that some men seemed to shy away from her, but she didn't know why. She couldn't see herself clearly enough to realize that she had too much: success, beauty, courage, and a self-confident air that verged on arrogance.

Fergus's house was situated in a discreetly expensive mews. He showed her into a luxuriously furnished living room, and excused himself.

He returned in ten minutes. "This is a map of Glenrie, the village on the mainland and here's the address of a man named Jimmy Orken. Give him this note from me and he'll take you over in his boat. The map of the island itself shows you where the house is, and I've put a cross where I think you'll find the eagles. And while I was upstairs I found this. I thought you'd like to see it."

He put a large wedding photograph into her hand. At the center stood the daintiest bride Sara had ever seen. Laurel Calvin had been a tiny, black-haired, fine-boned creature. In her frothy bridal gown she seemed almost fairylike. She was looking up at her bride-groom, who stood with one arm around her waist. His hand looked brutally large against the girl's delicate proportions. It was a hand that could kill without mercy, Sara thought.

Rorke Calvin had been almost a foot taller than his bride. He dominated the picture, not only with his height, but with the swarthy harshness of his face. Sara wondered how dark his deep-set eyes were in real life. The picture made them look totally black, with a cruel glitter.

She gave herself a little shake and tried not to be fanciful. Knowing that Rorke Calvin was a murderer was making her read things into his picture that probably weren't there. She was surely imagining that Laurel's glance at her husband contained a touch of fear, or that the ferocious possessiveness in his face amounted almost to a scowl. But there was no doubt he wasn't smiling as a bridegroom ought to. There was a brooding watchfulness in those black eyes.

Sara noticed his breadth of shoulder, the hint of lean, athletic hardness that the wedding suit imper-fectly concealed. He radiated power, both mentally and physically.

"He certainly looks like a dangerous man," she said at last.

"I know. I tried to warn Laurel, but she wouldn't listen."

"That's you, isn't it?" Sara asked, peering at the man who stood on Laurel's other side. "But there's something different about you."

"Probably my nose. It was straight in those days. That was before Rorke rearranged it. He broke three of my ribs, smashed my nose and left me unconscious, all because I dared to protest about the way he treated my sister."

"Wasn't he arrested?"

"He would have been if I'd had my way. But Laurel implored me not to press charges." He took the picture from her and handed her a brown sealed envelope. "Here's the key." Sara put it safely in her purse.

Fergus was studying her. "Now I know why I thought I knew your face," he said. "There was a magazine article about you that said you'd go anywhere and do anything for a picture. I can see it's true. But don't be too reckless, Sara. I'll worry about you in that wild place. Call me in a few days."

"I promise I'll call."

"Good. Then I'll drive you home."

Sara reached Farraway on a bright, breezy afternoon, two days later. She was tired from the long drive to the northwest coast of Scotland, and Jimmy Orken, a taciturn man in his forties, advised her to stay overnight in Glenrie. But she insisted on being taken over as soon as she'd stocked up with provisions.

It was late summer and the sun shone brilliantly, but once Jimmy's dinghy had put to sea Sara was aware of a nip in the air. She drank in the freshness, feeling it flood gloriously through her like wine. At last the horizon was broken by a black line that gradually resolved itself into steep cliffs. "That's Farraway," Jimmy told her.

Sara squinted, trying to make out details. "Are there cliffs all the way around?"

"Aye, there's no easy access to the island. It's as bleak a piece of earth as ever was. It's uninhabited because the land's too poor to farm. Nothing grows there but heather, and nothing lives there but animals."

As they drew closer the cliffs reared up, dark and forbidding. The sun's brilliance had dimmed to a pale, chill light, and there was suddenly a biting edge to the wind. Sara began to wonder if she'd have been wiser to wait until the next day to come. Jimmy had warned her that he'd have to leave almost at once, which meant getting her baggage to the house alone. But it was too late to worry about that now.

When they'd beached the boat in a small pebble cove, he helped her to haul her things up the path of the two hundred foot cliff. In addition to her suitcase there was the large metal case with her cameras and the box of provisions she'd bought in Glenrie. When the last box was brought up they rested to catch their breath. "Can you tell me which day I'm to fetch you?" Jimmy asked.

Sara shook her head. "I don't want to commit myself in case that's a good day for the eagles. You said you'd give me some flares."

"I've put them in with your provisions. I'm most likely to spot them either at morning or evening. You see over there?" he pointed to where the land rose steeply into a promontory. Darkness was beginning to fall and Sara had to peer. "That's the highest point on Farraway and it faces the mainland. Send up your flares from there and I'll see them. But keep well away from the edge. It's three hundred feet down to the rocks. A bad place, that one.''

Something in his voice made her look up sharply. ''Is that where...?''

''Aye, that's the place. The devil himself dragged the poor lassie up there and flung her down, may he rot in hell!''

''The devil himself,'' Sara savored the picturesque words.

''In this part of the world we say what we mean,'' Jimmy told her. ''That man was a devil. We used to see him in Glenrie sometimes when they were living on the island. We seldom saw her. He kept her shut up over there and he didn't like being asked about her. It was no surprise to anyone when he killed her.''

''I suppose there's no doubt that he did it?'' Sara queried. ''After all, the verdict was Not Proven.''

''If they'd known their business they'd have found him guilty. I'll be wishing you well.'' He rose and looked around at the bleak scrub and the distant moors blotched with dark shadows. ''Myself, I shouldn't like to be alone in this place.''

As soon as he'd left her Sara got to work briskly. She made the trip to the house in stages, carrying her suitcase and camera case a hundred yards, then going back for the provisions. A rest, a glance at the map by flashlight, then another hundred yards. By this means she arrived at the house after two hours, perspiring, exhausted and in poor humor.

Night had fallen now, but there was a good moon, and Sara could make out that it was a very large house with a Victorian look, sturdy and decorative.

She groped in her pocket for the envelope with the key and tore it open. She found the lock more by feel than sight, and to her relief the key turned without trouble.

It was completely dark inside. She used the flashlight to make her way down a long hall toward an open door; through it she could glimpse a sink and a gas stove. Two oil lamps stood in a corner, and when they were lit the kitchen took on a friendlier appearance.

The pantry was far better stocked than Fergus had led her to expect. She pushed her box of provisions inside, just as it was. The stove worked from cylinders of liquid gas. Sara put on some eggs to boil, took an oil lamp and went upstairs to investigate the bedrooms. Her feet echoed on the wooden floors and the great empty house seemed to groan with her progress. It was an old building, she reminded herself, and probably full of creaks and strange noises.

The first door she tried was locked. She went down the corridor, opening the other doors and glancing at the rooms. At the end she discovered a paneled door, larger than the others, which yielded easily. She went in and found herself standing in a corner room. It had windows on two sides, and by the brilliant moonlight she could make out a four-poster hung with curtains. She surveyed the room with delight, and when she found that it had its own bathroom she decided to sleep there.

She returned downstairs, but at the door to the kitchen she stopped, assailed by a sudden shattering sense of something *wrong*. It was as powerful as if a warning hand had pushed her back. For a moment she stood there, petrified. Then the moment passed as suddenly as it had come. She gave a shaky laugh at her own overactive imagination.

While she ate her eggs she studied the front door key, which was attached to a key ring of some heavy metal. The light was too poor to make out details, but she could tell that the metal was finely engraved.

She finished eating and carried her suitcase up to the bedroom. After changing sleepily into her night-gown, she climbed onto the high mattress, drew the curtains around her, and within less than a minute was dead to the world.

She was alert in an instant. She didn't know what had awoken her, but every nerve was screaming that something was amiss on the other side of the curtains. It was the same sensation that she'd felt in the kitchen, but now it was a hundred times more intense. She remained still, but despite the pounding of her heart the room was completely silent. The luminous dial of her watch showed that she'd been asleep an hour. She reached for the curtain, but froze before she'd even touched it, her throat contracted, stifling the scream that tried to escape.

In horror she watched the curtains slide open in one smooth motion.

Two

Beyond the curtains the room was flooded with moonlight. Silhouetted against it, stark and terrifying, loomed a large man. He stood motionless, his arms outstretched above his head where he'd slid the curtains aside, both the attitude and the stillness making him look colossal. Then, with incredible speed, he moved, reaching forward to grab Sara as she tried to wriggle away. The hand that closed about her wrist was strong as steel, ruthless and unbreakable. She felt her other wrist grasped and imprisoned with the first, and both were thrust high over her head, pinning her to the mattress. In this way her assailant could keep her helpless with his left hand while he groped for the oil lamp with his right.

Sara's fighting spirit came rushing back and she managed to raise her head a few inches, seeking to bite his arm, but the position left him too far out of reach.

She writhed frantically but her wrists were firmly imprisoned. Suddenly her throat relaxed. She managed to scream, partly in fear and partly in anger and frustration. He growled something unintelligible and gripped her hands more tightly.

"Keep still while I light the lamp." He turned up the wick of the oil lamp and struck a match against the sole of his shoe. Sara drew in her breath sharply as the match blazed for a moment and went out. They were in darkness again and her heart was thumping wildly, for in that brief second she'd recognized the features of the man before her.

"Rorke Calvin!" she whispered.

Another match flared and this time the wick caught. Rorke replaced the glass bell and turned to face her. Her heart almost stopped at the sight of the bleak, shadowed face. In this light it looked even more grim than it had in the wedding picture. Lines of savage experience had been scored into it. His mouth was firm to the point of hardness, and there was a black glint in his eyes. This was a man who'd already killed one woman on this very island. The thought made her newly conscious of the hand enclosing her wrists. He followed the flicker of her eyes and loosened his fingers. "Just keep still," he ordered curtly, "and don't give me any trouble."

She'd die rather than let him see her fear. "Yes, terrorizing women is a specialty of yours, isn't it?" she managed to say with spirit.

He grinned, a mirthless stretching of the mouth that frightened her more than his bleakness. "Of course, you know who I am, don't you, Sara? Fergus must've told you all about me."

"How do you know my name?" she gasped.

"It was on your driving license. I checked your things to find out who my unexpected guest was."

"Unexpected guest?"

"Haven't you understood yet that I was here long before you? I've been living in this house for months. I saw you coming and locked myself in the bedroom at the far end of the corridor."

So that was why she'd found that door locked. Shivers went up her spine at the thought of him sitting silently on the other side, biding his time.

"I wasn't too pleased at your intrusion," Rorke continued, "but that was before I worked out how you could be useful to me. Just how useful I'm not yet sure. It depends how big an impression you made on Fergus, but I think you probably did pretty well."

His gaze flickered over her in a way that made his meaning plain. Her nightgown was short and her struggles had made it ride up almost to the tops of her thighs. Where it covered her, it clung, revealing every line of her slim, curved body. She was embarrassingly aware how much the low neckline revealed of her full breasts. She grabbed the blanket and pulled it up until she was decently covered. "If you mean what I think you do—"

"I mean exactly that."

"Then you couldn't be more wrong. There's nothing like that between Fergus and me."

"I find that difficult to believe. Fergus only has one use for a beautiful woman. He doesn't usually go to these lengths for a private rendezvous, though. He sent you on ahead to open up the love nest, didn't he? How long before he follows you?"

"He isn't following me," she insisted desperately. "I'm not opening any 'love nest.' I'm here alone."

"He wouldn't have let you come to Farraway unless he meant to join you, and I want you to tell me how long I have to wait."

Rorke's voice was quiet but he spoke with a deadly undertone. With an effort she managed to reply steadily, "You'll wait forever, then, because he isn't coming."

For a moment his eyes glinted and she was frighteningly conscious of her helplessness. She was half-naked and completely at the mercy of this murderer. But although his expression remained unyielding, he shrugged. "It hardly matters. We'll just wait for him. Whenever he comes I'll be ready. I've waited a year. A few more days won't matter."

"If you want Fergus, why don't you just go and see him in London?" she demanded. "He certainly seemed anxious to see you, too."

Rorke gave a snort of laughter. "Is that what he's told you? I couldn't get to see Fergus if I took an army and a battering ram. He's not man enough to face me."

"How strange," she said scathingly. "He implied the same thing about you."

Rorke turned cold eyes on her. "Be careful Sara. We have to find a way of living together for the next few days and it isn't going to be easy. Don't make it worse."

"What makes you think I'm staying?"

"What makes you think you'll have any choice? You'll stay here with me, for as long as it takes to bring Fergus out in pursuit. Don't give me any trouble, and don't try my patience, because I'm not a patient man—as you may have heard."

She felt the ice take possession of her body, beginning with her heart and reaching out to her fingertips. She couldn't have moved at that moment if her life had depended on it. While she lay petrified, he walked out of the room, and a second later she heard the key turn in the lock.

Sara was up, showered and fully dressed when Rorke came to her door the next morning. She hadn't slept a wink since he'd left her the night before. She'd lain there, staring into the darkness, trying to take in the full horror of her situation. Farraway was uninhabited except for herself and a man with blood on his hands. She could scream the place down. The mainland was five miles away and no one would help her.

Her bedroom was flooded with bright morning sunlight now. Through the two tall windows she could see the bleak beauty of the island, with the green-brown, windswept landscape stretching away until it rose into rock-strewn hills.

She was looking out the window when she heard footsteps in the corridor and the sound of the key turning, and in another moment the door opened.

It was her first clear view of him, and now she understood why he'd seemed like a giant the night before. He was well over six foot, with broad shoulders and a muscular torso that tapered to narrow hips encased in faded old jeans. Once his shirt might have been green, but it, too, was old and faded to an indeterminate color. He'd left it open to the waist, showing the thick dark brown hair that covered his chest, thinning slightly as it approached his flat stomach, and vanished into the confining leather belt.

His sleeves were pushed back, showing the same dark hair on his forearms and the backs of his hands. Beneath it, the skin had the tan of a man who spent much time outdoors during all seasons. It was the tan of wind and weather as much as sun, and with the athletic leanness of his body it confirmed that he really had lived here for long, hard months. Sara enjoyed solitude, but the thought of that brooding, embittered presence keeping silent vigil in this bleak place left her speechless.

His nose was very slightly hooked in a way that reminded her of the eagles she'd come here to find. His coloring was the same, too, for a beam of sunlight struck the rich brown of his hair, highlighting a touch of red that wasn't noticeable in shadow. She suppressed a shudder. The eagle was a bird of prey, pitiless in its pursuit and capture of its victim. The momentary resemblance reminded her that she was the victim now, helpless in the grip of deadly claws.

"Good, you're ready," he observed. "Let's go downstairs."

He stood back for her to pass. As they turned the corner of the stairs she glanced quickly at the front door. Rorke Calvin's sharp eyes detected her movement, and he told her it was locked.

As soon as she reached the kitchen she knew why she'd sensed something wrong the night before. If the house had been empty for over a year the kitchen should've been covered by a thick layer of dust, but everything was spotless. "I've looked at the supplies you brought," Rorke told her. "I was glad to see some bacon and eggs. Mine ran out a week ago. I'll have two of each."

She stared at him. "Are you seriously expecting me to cook for you?"

"I don't see why not. You'd have made breakfast for yourself. Just put in some extra."

"I won't do it," she snapped. "I'm not your servant and you can get your own food—"

She broke off with a gasp of alarm as he walked quickly toward her. She was five-foot-six but he was at least eight inches taller, with a muscular build and large hands. When he pulled her against him she tried to struggle, but she was trapped in the circle of his arms, pressed so closely to his hard body that she could feel its warmth through the layers of material. "Once and for all, Sara, you'd better understand your position," he said firmly. "You're my prisoner. That means I give the orders."

"And you think I'm meekly going to obey? Never!" she shouted, spurred on to defy him by a rising tide of rage. "I am *not* your prisoner," she added with slow emphasis, glaring up into his face.

Suddenly he smiled with genuine amusement. It was so unexpected that her heart started to thump. For the first time she realized that his mouth hadn't originally been hard. Nature had made it generous and full, with an unmistakable sensuality. For a moment she glimpsed the attractive man he must have once been, a man who possessed the elusive charm that could turn a woman's head. It had nothing to do with appearance, although he had more than his share of good looks. It was more to do with an unruly glint in his eyes as they laughed down at her. "I've got to hand it to you for stubbornness," he said. "In just what sense do you think you're not my prisoner? Can you get away from me now?"

She glared up at him, trying to ignore the clean, masculine scent that filled her nostrils, and the hard warmth of his body against the length of her own. "You have no right to do this," she choked.

"You barged into my territory, Sara," he observed mildly. "I didn't ask you to come. Now that you're here we just have to try and be civil to each other for as long as it takes."

She knew it was useless to struggle, but rage made her do it anyway. She twisted with sudden determination, trying to kick herself free. The writhing movement against his body caused a frisson to go through her that she tried to ignore. His expression changed to one of shock, and the next moment he released her so abruptly that she almost fell. She was shaking but she found the strength to say bitterly, "It isn't my habit to be civil to murderers."

Sheer surprise held him silent. She saw anger in his expression, but also something that might have been curiosity. "There aren't many people who'd have the guts to say that to my face," he said, almost to himself.

Sara's temper was hot and reckless. It could carry her away and make her talk wildly. She could feel it taking possession of her now, and she let it happen because she was determined not to knuckle under to this man. "Why shouldn't I say it?" she blazed. "I'm not afraid of you. You're not the first animal I've been trapped with, but at least other animals only kill for food, not greed."

Her words seemed to hang in the still air. Rorke's face was startlingly pale. After a moment he said quietly, "You're either very brave or very stupid." And with that he turned and walked out.

Sara kept her eyes on the door, breathing deeply. She supposed she'd been stupid, but she couldn't regret having struck a blow that had taken him aback.

She began hauling food out of the supply box she'd brought last night. Then she stopped and stared. She'd forgotten about Jimmy Orken's flares which were still at the bottom of the box where he'd put them. By a lucky chance Rorke had looked no further than the food on top. If she could escape from the house she could send them up. Quickly she seized a dry cloth, wrapped them in it and pushed them out of sight beneath the lowest shelf. Her heart beat with exhilaration. She'd won this round. Sooner or later he'd drop his guard and she'd get out.

She started the breakfast, working mechanically while she brooded on her problems. When she looked up she found Rorke standing in the doorway. She hadn't heard him, and now she wondered how long he'd been there. He was watching her, frowning as if something had disconcerted him. His face was still pale and he looked like he'd had to fight to recover his composure, but he didn't speak as he joined her at the table.

While they ate, her mind was occupied with a thousand enjoyable fantasies of revenge. The last man who'd managed to intimidate her had been her father, a selfish bully who'd forced her to leave school early to take care of him after her mother died. She'd allowed him to run her life for a year, seething with resentment over her lost opportunities.

At last she'd rebelled, leaving his house and kicking the dust of the small provincial town off her feet. She'd never gone back. Without a penny to her name, she'd made her way to London and gotten a job in a photographic studio. She'd earned peanuts and slept in the studio, always on call, but she learned the trade. By the time she was twenty she'd decided, with outrageous confidence, that it was time she set up in business for herself. She descended on her bank and emerged an hour later with the loan she needed. The enchanted bank manager never knew what hit him.

With no female relatives to advise her, all Sara knew about handling men had developed out of her own experience. Sooner or later every man turned into either her father or her bank manager, to be dealt with by aggression or charm, whichever seemed the most likely to succeed.

Now she found herself confronted by a man against whom both her trusty weapons were worthless, but where belligerence and beauty failed, a little dissimulating might work wonders. "I don't see how you've managed here for months," she remarked as casually as she could. "How do you get all the supplies?"

"From the mainland."

"Then how can you believe that no one knows you're here? The whole world must know by now."

"The whole world would know if I was fool enough to go into Glenrie," he agreed. "But I'm not, I take my boat seventy miles down the coast. There's a little cove where a friend leaves supplies for me. I go in at night, switching off the engine while I'm still at sea and rowing the last two miles. After I collect the supplies, I row back out to sea, start the engine and return here. No one sees me, and even if they did it's always too dark for my face to be recognized.

"I'm telling you all this because I don't want you to delude yourself that there's going to be a rescue. Only my friend knows I'm here, and he'll go to the stake before he gives me away.''

She should've realized he'd think of everything. After a whle she asked, ''When you went through my things last night, did you look at the metal box?''

''Yes, I saw the cameras.''

''Then you know I'm a photographer. I'm doing a book on rare birds and I came here for shots of the golden eagles. If Fergus and I were using this place as a romantic hideaway, why on earth would I bring all those cameras?'' Sarcasm infused her voice. ''Or do you think I was planning to take pornographic pictures by remote control?''

He grinned. ''No, you're here for the eagles. So what?''

''So what? What about your theory that I came to open up the love nest? I'm here to photograph eagles.''

''I accept that, but it doesn't prove Fergus isn't coming,'' he said. ''You wouldn't be the first photographer to combine business with pleasure.''

''Then I suggest you have a look at the wardrobe I've brought with me,'' she exclaimed, exasperated. ''When you see my clothes you just might ask yourself why I didn't choose something a bit more glamorous to impress Fergus with.''

Rorke shrugged. ''In this place? Besides, he'd have your clothing off in five minutes.'' Sara drew in her breath indignantly, but before she could speak Rorke raised a hand to silence her. ''Look, you're wasting your time. I don't give a damn why you're here. All I care about is that Fergus will follow you.''

''But he—''

''He will! One way or another, he's coming to Farraway. Maybe you didn't know that. Perhaps he's saving it for a surprise. But even if he hadn't planned to, what do you suppose he'll do when you're discovered missing? Just sit there? I don't think so. He'll be up here searching for you before anyone else does.''

Her heart lurched. His words had brought back to her the memory of Fergus saying, ''I'll worry about you in that wild place. Don't forget to call me....''

She'd left Fergus her card, so he'd call her apartment when he didn't hear from her, and when the phone stayed unanswered long enough, what then? Surely he'd just tell Jimmy Orken to check? Fergus was a busy man. He'd never make the trip himself, would he?

Sara was seized by inspiration. The words that came out of her mouth next seemed to shape themselves without conscious help from her brain. ''Fergus will only come if he gets the signal.''

''What signal?'' Rorke demanded sharply.

''We didn't know how long it would take me to get the house ready. So we arranged that I'd go back to the mainland and call him, telling him to come. He won't budge from London until he hears from me.''

She could hear her own heart thumping as Rorke stared at her through narrowed eyes. ''Very clever, Sara,'' he said softly. ''Of course, you'd be more clever to stop playing games with me.''

''It's true,'' she insisted desperately. ''He won't come unless I call him.''

''I don't believe you. You invented this arrangement just now, and for someone in a tight corner it isn't a bad try. Even if it *is* true, when that call doesn't come he'll chase up here to discover why. But at least you've admitted that you're expecting Fergus.''

"I'm not expecting him," she said through gritted teeth. "He won't be here if you wait from now until kingdom come. What do you want? Why is it so important that Fergus come to Farraway?"

"That's not your concern, Sara," he told her coldly. "And if you're wise, you'll stay out of it."

"How can I stay out of it when you've dragged me into it?" she demanded angrily.

"Then let's say I want you to keep to the sidelines. Your part in this is going to be a small one and when you've played it you can go. But it's better if you don't ask any questions." He rose abruptly to his feet. "If you've finished eating you can go back upstairs."

"Don't tell me I'm going to be spared doing the washing up?" she demanded sarcastically.

"You're less trouble if you're locked in your room. And somehow I feel you're going to give me a lot of trouble."

"How inconsiderate of me," she snapped.

He grinned faintly. "Come on."

He walked behind her as they climbed the stairs, and came into the bedroom with her. "Until last night I slept in here myself," he said. "I've let you have it because it's on the landward side of the house. If you'd been facing the sea, I daresay you'd have started playing tricks with lights."

"I daresay," she echoed ironically.

He went out and locked her in. A few minutes later she heard the slam of the front door. She could see him through her window walking off toward the hills, a gun tucked under his arm. She pulled her powerful binoculars out of her case to study his retreating form and a sick feeling overtook her. Rorke was carrying a

double-barreled shotgun. With every step the brilliant sun danced off its barrel.

Now she knew why he was waiting for Fergus, a
man he hated, a man he couldn't reach any other way.
Rorke Calvin wanted revenge. But for Fergus he might
have gotten away with the suicide story. He wasn't in
prison where he ought to be, but he was a marked
man, and his revenge was so important to him that
he'd sweep aside anything and anyone who stood in his
way.

She *must* get to the promontory with those flares. It
was the only way to save Fergus's life.

She began to study her room. There was no escape
through the window, which looked out onto a small
greenhouse with a glass roof. The wall immediately
below the window was smooth. Sara was a reasonably good climber, but she knew that to attempt to go
down that way would be madness.

She discovered that the door locked with an old-
fashioned key, and lay down to examine the crack between the door and the floor. Her heart began to beat
a little faster. The crack was just large enough to allow the key to be pulled through. Hardly daring to
believe her luck she rummaged in the wardrobe for a
sheet and slipped one corner of it under the door immediately below the keyhole. Then she took out her
long-tailed comb and probed in the lock until she
heard the key slide out and fall on the other side.

She nearly cheered aloud. It was an old trick, but
Rorke Calvin had plainly never heard of it. Holding
her breath, she began to pull the sheet gently toward
her. In a few minutes she'd be out of this place.

A small sound told her that she'd rejoiced too soon.
Squinting frantically under the door, she saw that the

far end of the key was a fraction too thick to pass under the door. She jiggled it in every direction, but
nothing worked. She could have screamed with frustration.

It was evening by the time Rorke returned. Sara
heard the front door slam and braced herself for his
arrival at her door. But it was another two hours before she heard his approach. She'd removed the sheet,
but the key still lay on the floor, and she ground her
teeth at the thought of how he'd find it and guess
about her fruitless escape attempt.

She heard the slight scrape as he picked up the key,
followed by silence. Then the sound of a soft chuckle
reached her. She found herself thinking it was one of
the most attractive sounds she'd ever heard, rich with
warmth and kindly humor, things that were alien to
the man holding her prisoner. There was something
cockeyed about a world where a killer possessed a
laugh like that.

When he'd opened the door he just stood there,
grinning. "I'd have bet money that you'd think of that
one," he said.

"I'm glad to have given you some amusement," she
snapped.

"Don't be angry. Think how bored you'd have been
without a way of passing the time." He indicated for
her to leave the room ahead of him. "I know how it
feels being locked up."

"Next thing you'll expect me to be grateful to you
for allowing me to fix supper," she snapped sarcastically.

"I've already fixed supper. I didn't think I could
face another of your meals."

A delicious aroma of rabbit stew was coming from the kitchen, and Sara discovered she was ravenously hungry. "I shot a few rabbits this afternoon," Rorke explained as they sat down.

"With a double-barreled shotgun?" Sara demanded. "Isn't that a little high-powered for rabbits?"

"Eat your supper," Rorke advised. They ate in silence for a few minutes. The stew was delicious. After a while he said, "I went to the cliffs overlooking the bay. There was no sign of anyone coming, but I suppose it's too soon for that."

"Oh, God." she muttered. "Look, where do you get this idea from, anyway? Just because I'm here? That's ridiculous. I asked Fergus to let me come to Farraway for a few days to photograph the eagles, and he agreed. He was doing me a simple favor, no more than that."

"Does he often do you 'simple favors'?"

"I only knew him a couple of hours."

Rorke raised an eyebrow. "You mean he was doing you favors that fast? You must have made a big impression on him. What did you do, pick him up?"

"That depends what you call a pickup," she hedged.

"I call it what happens when a woman fixes a man in her sights and goes all out to get him."

Dismayed, she considered this definition, which fitted her own actions so uncannily well. "It...wasn't quite like that."

"Which means it was exactly like that," he remarked dryly.

"All I wanted was his permission to come here."

"For which you could have called his secretary."

"I had, that afternoon. But when I bumped into him at a party in the evening I seized my chance."

"What did you do?"

She sighed. "I spilled my drink and pretended it was his fault."

Rorke threw back his head and laughed. It was like the chuckle she'd heard outside her door, warm and vibrantly attractive. She tried to shut her ears to it. "Look," she said, "I let him take me to dinner so that we could talk privately, but that was all."

"And he said, 'Certainly, Sara, by all means have the freedom of the island,'" Rorke put in ironically.

"No, he refused at first, because of his sister's memory, but then he changed his mind. He said it was what she'd have wanted. It was just an act of kindness."

"Sara, listen. I know Fergus Drummond much better than you seem to think. He's a ruthless self-seeker. He never does favors unless he can see what's in it for him. I don't know what I find more laughable, the thought of him moved by sentimental memories of his sister, or the thought of him doing an act of kindness."

Sara shrugged. "Well, I've told you what happened. I can't make you believe me."

"Tell me something else. How did you recognize me that first night?"

"Fergus showed me your picture."

"Which he just happened to be carrying with him?"

"No," she conceded unwillingly, seeing what he was forcing her to admit. "I went to his house to get the key, but I was only there a few minutes."

She wondered if he'd heard the last few words. When she'd mentioned the key Rorke had stiffened and his expression grew hard. After a moment he reached into his pocket. "This key?" he asked, putting it on the table between them.

"That's right." She picked it up and studied the coin that formed the key ring. Now that she could look at it properly, she saw it was a medallion. From its weight it might have been solid gold. The intricate decoration seemed to be a pattern of clasped hands, and around the edge were engraved the words, *Nec tecum possum vivere nec sine te.* "It's beautiful," she murmured. "It looks like an antique."

"It is."

She held it closer to the light, turning it between reverent fingers. "Strange..." She was almost talking to herself.

"What's strange?"

"Well, Fergus." she said vaguely. "Somehow I don't associate him with something like this." The truth was that beneath Fergus's pleasant manners she'd detected a touch of crassness, but she wasn't going to admit that to his enemy.

Rorke looked at her curiously. "That's very astute of you," he observed. "It's a pity you don't see the rest of him so clearly. Money is all he cares about and all he knows about."

"Then how come he has such a lovely thing?"

"It belonged to my wife. It was the first gift I ever gave her."

Surprise nearly made her drop it. "You?"

"I never saw it again after she died, but I assumed Fergus had stolen it. Evidently I was right. Did he tell you what the inscription meant?"

"No," she said slowly. "I never saw it until now. He gave me the key in a sealed envelope. I didn't open it until I arrived last night." She saw his look of disbelief and added, "If I'd seen something like this attached I'd have taken it off first." She placed the key ring onto the table and walked past him into the hall where she'd hung her coat. She rummaged in the pocket for a moment, then returned to the kitchen. "Here," she said. "This is the envelope it was in."

He took it from her and studied it. Sara had ripped open the side and the flap was still sealed. "You could've had anything in here," he said, but his voice was uncertain.

"But look at the way it's creased. You can see the outline of the key ring from carrying it in my pocket." She fitted the key back into the envelope and the creases fell into place. "What difference does it make, anyway?" she asked when he still didn't speak.

"No real difference, perhaps. I just don't like finding something of my wife's in your possession."

"As far as I knew, it was just a key," she said.

Rorke was frowning and there was the same disconcerted look she'd seen on his face that morning when she'd defied him. "I guess I have to believe you," he said at last.

"Then believe me, too, when I say Fergus isn't coming here."

"And let you go? I can't. You'd go straight to him and tell him I was here. When you don't show up, he'll come looking."

"Or send the police."

"No, he won't do that. Don't hope for it, Sara. Fergus doesn't want the police nosing around this place again. He'll come here himself."

"And then what?"

His eyes became cold. "I told you before that we'll get through the next few days better if you don't ask any questions. What happens between Fergus and me is none of your concern, and it's going to stay that way."

That night Sara didn't go straight to bed, but sat at the window brooding over what she'd discovered. Rorke had asked her if Fergus had translated the inscription on the gold coin, assuming that she couldn't do so herself. It was an assumption that had cost him a point in their duel. Sara was good at languages. She'd studied Latin at school and retained enough to understand that the words meant, "I can live neither with you nor without you."

She knew now that Rorke Calvin had loved his wife with a love that was half hate—the kind of love that could have made him kill.

Three

———

Over the next few days they slipped into a kind of routine. Sara took over the cooking without further protest because that way Rorke was less likely to discover the flares hidden in the pantry. She watched constantly for a chance to escape with them, but it never came.

She found the house modern in some respects and primitive in others. There was running water, of a kind. First it had to be pumped up from the well in the yard and fed into large containers. The cooking gas cylinders were among the supplies Rorke brought over from the mainland.

At the back of the house stood a generator that could have supplied electricity, but Rorke had deliberately allowed it to run down so that no carelessly turned-on light could be visible from the sea. So the refrigerator was useless, and when darkness fell there

were only candles and oil lamps for lighting. Food was
kept cool in a brick hut just outside the kitchen and the
nonperishable supplies were stored in the indoor pantry.

Sometimes he would lock her in her room and go
out carrying a large pair of binoculars. She guessed
that he was going to the cliff to watch the water for any
sign of Fergus. After a few hours he'd return, his
expression grim. He never spoke to her about these
trips, or the hours he spent waiting. Sara wondered
how long it would take him to face the fact that Fergus wasn't coming, and what he'd do when he did.

While they waited they lived a life of incongruous
domesticity. In this respect Rorke was a model companion, doing his share of the chores, although there
were often practical reasons for it. Scraps were
brought to a compost heap outside the kitchen. Rorke
always did this himself, thus affording her no excuse
for getting even a few steps outside the house.

Sara had always had an instinctive affinity with animals that had often enabled her to charm creatures
into coming to her, making her very successful at her
job. Even in the midst of her troubles, that empathy
asserted itself. On her first day she'd noticed a blackbird perched on a nearby bush, watching her hope-
fully. She'd left some crumbs on the sill, and had later
found them gone.

He'd been there every day since and she began to
keep a few scraps for him. One day while Rorke was
outside, disposing of the remains of lunch, Sara spread
her offering on the sill. The blackbird considered it but
didn't move. "Here," she urged, holding out a hand
with some crumbs in the palm.

The bird tilted his head and regarded her, bright-eyed.

"You'll eat it the minute my back's turned," she chided him. "How about now?"

The blackbird relented as far as flying down to perch on the sill at a safe distance from her. "Come on," she coaxed, reaching a little further toward him. He stayed where he was, but winked an eye at her. His ridiculous solemnity made her laugh aloud and he immediately took flight back to the bush. Sara turned back into the room to find Rorke watching her, grinning. "He'll tease you like that endlessly," he said. "It's taken me a year to get him as far as that windowsill."

His smile was pleasant, even charming, and she was immediately wary. She shrugged and assumed the indifferent tone that had proved the most effective armor. "How disappointing. I thought he was coming here because of me."

The smile vanished from his face. "Talking of food, we could do with some more fresh meat. I'm going to get some rabbits this afternoon."

"I'll come with you," she said quickly.

He scowled. "No."

"Look, I haven't set foot out of this house for three days. I need some fresh air and exercise. I can't stand being locked up in that room. You can't imagine—" she checked herself at the ironic look on his face.

"Quite," he agreed, answering her hesitation rather than her words. "I don't need to imagine. I spent several weeks behind bars while I was awaiting my trial."

"Well, then, you know why I need to get out."

He shrugged. "All right."

She really did long for a change of scene, but she also hoped to obtain a picture of the island that would be useful when she escaped. Looking up, she caught a glint in Rorke's eye that suggested he knew what she was up to.

The trip out was both a frustration and a pleasure. The frustration arose from the fact that Rorke made her leave her cameras behind, claiming they'd be an encumbrance. The pleasure sprang from some of the most savagely beautiful scenery she'd ever seen. Rocky crags rose in the distance where, she guessed, the eagles nested. But she was too far away to discern details. In between stretched miles of bleak moorland, mostly tinted green-brown, but sometimes enlivened by brilliant purple heather. The first time she saw it, Sara stopped dead and exclaimed, "Oh, how glorious!"

"Yes, isn't it?" Rorke agreed. "That's one thing this place can grow. There's more in the other direction, pink, white, yellow. At one time the house was full of heather..." His voice trailed off. "Don't hang behind," he told her abruptly.

It was a difficult afternoon. Rorke had set his mind on getting two rabbits, and in the end did, but it took a long time to catch sight of even the slightest movement. By the time he'd finished they'd been walking for hours, the light was fading, and they were both cold, tired and hungry. They tramped home in silence, and when the house came into sight Sara discovered she was actually glad to see it, something she wouldn't have thought possible.

"Wait," Rorke said suddenly. "There's something over there. If I can get it, it'll save another trip out."

He raised his gun and aimed it at what appeared to be a white powder puff darting across the ground in the distance. There was an explosion and the puff disappeared. They hurried over to the spot, but there was nothing there. "Damn!" Rorke muttered, looking around him. "I shouldn't have tried in this light."

Sara shrugged. "So you missed it. Let it go for heaven's sake!"

"No, I didn't miss it. Look, there's a spot of blood on the ground. I hit that animal, but not fatally." He stood up and looked around in all directions. "Can I trust you to stay here?"

"Why? What are you going to do?"

"I've got to find the rabbit. It must be in agony. I can't just leave it to die like that. I won't be long, because it can't have gotten far, but if I don't have your word to keep still you'll have to come with me."

Sara's answer was to flop down onto the ground and sit there, looking up at him defiantly. "Do I look as if I'm going anywhere?" she demanded.

"All right, just stay there." He turned on his heel and left her.

Sara sat where she'd flopped, feeling cold and weariness in every corner of her being. This was where she ought to escape, but escape was useless unless she could get the flares, and Rorke had the key to the house. So she stayed there, trying to sort out her impressions of a man who could kill his wife yet take the trouble to save a rabbit unnecessary suffering.

None of the details about him fitted together, she reflected. He was a killer and he dressed like a tramp, yet his voice was that of an educated man, a rich bass that under other circumstances she'd have thought beautiful. Even his accent had surprised her. She'd assumed he must be a Scot like Fergus, but he sounded as English as herself.

Fergus had insisted he was after Laurel's money, yet Rorke's first gift to her had been an antique medallion with an ambiguous message. If he was a fortune hunter he'd gone about it very subtly.

Sara caught herself thinking "if", and started. She'd drifted into believing that nothing about Rorke Calvin was the way it seemed, and that was dangerous.

Rorke returned thirty minutes later with the dead rabbit, to find her half asleep. "I'm disappointed in you," he mocked as he hauled her to her feet. "I'd expected a heroic dash for the shore."

"Get lost," she said grumpily. It was all she had the energy for.

He grinned. "Let's head for home."

Later that evening he skinned the rabbits, raising an eyebrow at the sight of Sara's shudder. "For a wildlife photographer you're remarkably squeamish."

"I take pictures of animals, I don't dissect them," she replied shortly.

"An artist, not a scientist, hmm?"

"Yes," she agreed, surprised. "I do think of what I do as an art. I try to show the beauty in the wild."

"But animals also kill," he pointed out. "Do you avoid representing that because it isn't beautiful?"

"Of course not. I've taken pictures of lions devouring a zebra, and seals hunting penguins. It's part of nature, but..." She stopped and found Rorke's eyes on her.

"Why don't you finish what you have to say?" he asked quietly.

"Animals are still beautiful when they kill," she said. "Human beings aren't. That's what makes us unique."

He went on with his work and didn't look at her as he asked his next question. "What exactly did Fergus tell you about me, Sara?"

"That you killed your wife on Farraway, and the court found your case Not Proven."

"Yes," he agreed bitterly. "Scotland is unique in that little nicety. In any other country they'd have had to declare me innocent. Up here they want it both ways." There was a note of brooding to his voice. "They let your body go but keep your soul in bondage. I've had people in shops refuse to serve me, and doors slammed in my face. I didn't only come to the island because of Fergus, although he's the main reason. I also chose this life because when the world makes you an outcast it's easier to live like one. After a while it becomes difficult to think of yourself as anything else."

He wasn't looking at Sara, and she felt he'd forgotten her presence. His gaze was fixed on some distant world where there was only suffering, and for a moment his eyes were filled with a bleak misery that shocked her.

It was true, she reflected. If Rorke had been tried in England, the lack of final proof would have forced the court to declare him Not Guilty. There was only Fergus's word and he might have been mistaken. "Fergus says he saw you do it," she declared. "He says he heard your wife pleading with you not to hurt her."

"Yes, I know his version. I heard it in the dock. It made a touching story."

"Are you saying it's not true?"

He grew still. "Would there be any point in my saying it? I've said it so often. Somehow I don't see you being the first person to believe me."

She thought of the sun winking off the barrel of his shotgun, and was amazed at herself for having thought him innocent for a moment. "Considering that you're planning to commit another murder, neither do I," she agreed ironically.

"Another—I've told you I won't hurt you."

"I don't mean me, I mean Fergus. That's why you're waiting for him, isn't it?"

"No," he snapped. "I have something else in mind."

"Sure you have," she said scornfully.

It was on the tip of his tongue to say that he didn't have to defend himself to her. But equally strong was the impulse to do just that. "Don't push me, Sara," he said finally, "I've never meant you any harm, but I'm not a safe man to provoke."

All her senses told her it was true. In the light from the oil lamps she could see that Rorke's face was livid. She caught the ragged note in his voice, and the air about her seemed to vibrate with the atmosphere of a man at the end of his tether. But she was being driven by a demon. She wanted to hear him say positively that he hadn't killed his wife. Then she might begin to understand the contradictions in Rorke Calvin—or she might hurl his words back in his teeth. She didn't know yet, but she wanted to hear what he'd say. "What is it you want with Fergus if you aren't going to kill him?" she demanded.

"I want him to confess."

She stared. "Are you trying to say that it was Fergus who threw her over?"

"It was Fergus who *drove* her over. He drove her to suicide. I told them that at the trial but I couldn't show them the motive. Just let me have him to myself up here and I can get all I need to clear my name."

Sara thought of the kindly, genial Fergus. Then she looked at the man before her, tense and racked with some pain that made his face haggard. Which of them was telling the truth? Why should she believe anything Rorke Calvin said? The court hadn't believed him. But, she remembered, they hadn't entirely found against him, either.

"You don't believe me, do you?" he demanded, and there was a new bitterness in his voice. "You've heard the story of the sainted brother, trying to save his sister from the monster who married her for her money, and you've fallen for it, as they all have. What no one's ever tried to explain is why, if I was such a devil, Laurel married me in the first place."

"I suppose you managed to make her fall in love with you," Sara ventured.

He gave a harsh laugh. "No, I didn't *make* her fall in love with me. Love can't be had that way. I know because I've tried. My wife never loved me. Now let's call this subject closed."

"No, please tell me about it," Sara insisted. "If she didn't love you why—"

"I said the subject's closed," he interrupted her coldly.

"But a moment ago you complained that I didn't believe you."

"Then I was a fool. It doesn't matter what you believe," he snapped.

She knew it was useless to ask further. Rorke had once again closed himself off from the world. He'd reached out briefly to communicate with her, but he'd revealed more than he meant to and now he was retreating defensively.

Rorke kept his face averted from her. He was furious with himself for having yielded to the impulse to seek her understanding. He'd been so long without warmth or kindness that existence in that cold place had become natural to him. Now this woman had barged into his life, and the painfully erected barriers that protected him had trembled with the shock. Even as an enemy she brought with her a breath of the outside world where there was human contact and the sound of voices.

Her own voice was deep and husky, full of vibrant femininity, and the fact that he'd always heard it filled with scorn hadn't disguised its beauty. He'd armored himself against the world's rejection, but Sara Tancred had found a chink in that armor. She was his prisoner, yet she could keep her self-possession while provoking him to lose his. That was a challenge to the bitter pride that had sustained him through eighteen hellish months.

On their first day together he'd held her close to him, meaning only to show how easily he could overcome her, and so make her less of a nuisance. But as he'd pressed her slim, curved body next to his he'd known he was doing something more dangerous to himself than to her. He'd looked down at her eyes, blazing with contempt, and seen how incredibly blue they were. He'd had a long moment to take in the perfect skin, flushed with anger, and the generous mouth whose soft fullness no amount of anger could destroy.

He'd tried to push aside forbidden thoughts that were a distraction from his purpose. But when she struggled furiously against him, a jolt of fire had gone through his body, warning him that he didn't dare fight her this way. Fear had made him snatch his hands away, and since then he'd avoided touching her except briefly.

But keeping his distance couldn't make him less aware of the lithe, graceful ease of her movements, or the way the column of her neck rose like a lily from the open collar of her shirt. It was possible to look away from the sight of her worn jeans hugging her outline, but not to banish the picture from his mind, or prevent it tormenting him. If he could he'd have obliterated not only that memory but also the far more dangerous one of her as he'd seen her today, tempting the blackbird. While she was unconscious of him her smile had been delightful. Her voice had sounded tender and free of strain, as he'd never heard it before, and her chuckle had held a rich warmth that broke into his solitary hell like music.

Then she'd turned and seen him, and her chill, wary mask had been hastily replaced. For a dreadful moment it was as if every door that had ever been closed against him had been slammed in his face once again.

She was like no other woman, not only because of her beauty and the self-sufficiency that had brought her alone to Farraway, but also because of an unconscious pride in her demeanor that separated her from the rest of the world. Tonight her derision had gotten under his skin again, luring him to reach out tentative hands to her, and he'd regretted it at once. But the temptation remained to discover the woman beneath the arrogant surface. Something stirred in his loins at

the thought of breaking through her defenses, searing
her with desire until her naked flesh trembled against
his. What would he see in her eyes when she'd met her
match and knew it?

He worked on, his head bent because he couldn't
risk looking at her lest she see his thoughts in his face.

Sara stayed where she was, watching Rorke, wishing he'd look up. She was disconcerted by what she'd
heard, and even more confused by her own reactions.
He'd hinted that he'd struggled to make his wife love
him, but had never won her heart. The thought, *She
must have been mad,* had flitted through Sara's mind
before she could stop it.

The idea of this remote man emerging from behind
his barriers to reach out yearningly to a woman was
intriguing but unlikely. Then she remembered the agony in his face before he'd averted it, and she felt a
stirring of pity. She'd seen such a look in the eyes of
animals, wounded past help, lashing out in their torment until their suffering was mercifully ended—as
Rorke had ended the rabbit's suffering this afternoon. But there was no such release for him.

She was so absorbed in her reverie that it was some
time before she realized that he'd taken his eyes off her
for longer than ever before. A chance had fallen into
her hands, and she blamed herself for almost missing
it. Moving slowly and silently, she edged toward the
door and out into the hall. Then she began to run up
the stairs. She heard his exclamation of anger and the
sound of him pursuing her, but she had gotten a good
head start.

She reached her door with enough time to snatch the
key from the outside, dart into the room and thrust the

key back into the lock. She turned it just before Rorke's weight crashed against the panels.

She was locked in again, but now there was all the difference in the world. This time she had the key and was in control. There was a primitive satisfaction in hearing Rorke's bellow of frustrated rage, and the sound of his fist slamming repeatedly on the panels. The heavy oak door shuddered under the impact, but it held.

"Sara, open this door."

"What for? So that you can lock me in again?" she yelled back. "I'm in now. I might as well stay in."

"If you think I'm letting you keep that key—"

"Unless you can beat the door down, you can't stop me."

A hail of blows on the oak panels was the answer to this. Sara watched them vibrating and shuddered to think of the power in Rorke's hands. She clenched her fists, her heart thumping painfully. At last the pounding stopped and was succeeded by an almost equally nerve-racking silence. It was absolute, and it went on and on until she wanted to scream. She pressed her ear against the door, but there wasn't a sound. The temptation to put her head out into the corridor was almost overwhelming, but she resisted it.

At last she went to bed and stretched out on top of the quilt. She meant only to close her eyes for a moment, but she fell asleep at once.

She awoke with a start. It was completely dark and she saw by the glow of her watch that it was two in the morning. She crept to the door, excitement rising in her. Now was her chance to get out and leave the house by a downstairs window. She could take the flares and lie low until dawn broke and Jimmy would be watch-

ing. If she could escape without Rorke's knowledge it
would be hours before he looked for her. Holding her
breath, she eased the door open a few inches.

Moonlight poured into the corridor from a window, showing Rorke stretched out on the floor, right
across her doorway with his back to her. She stood
petrified, steeling herself to step over him. But before
she could move Rorke turned swiftly and reached his
hand out to stop her. Sara just saw the gleam in his
eyes before she backed into the room and slammed the
door again.

She stayed frozen at the door. The silence was so
intense that she could hear the faintest sound from the
other side, including Rorke's breathing. She listened
as it changed into the slow rhythm of sleep, but she
didn't dare take another chance. After a long hesitation she returned to bed.

Rorke was in hell. He was chasing after something
that constantly eluded him. A thousand times he
nearly caught it, but it slipped through his fingers.
Horror shook him, for he knew he was coming to a
place from which there'd be no turning back.

Then he was on a high peak, buffeted by winds. His
wife's face danced before him. He reached out to grasp
her but he could touch nothing. Yet her face was still
there, demented with fear, shrieking out her terror and
distrust, pleading with him to come no nearer, to let
her be.

Suddenly he was alone. There was nothing but the
wind and the sound of the distant sea, and the darkness that would last forever. He screamed again and
again, but no sound came.

Four

It was light when Sara awoke. She went to the window and saw that dawn had broken, although there was no sun and a pearly gray sheen seemed to lie over the landscape. The sky was full of clouds, and wherever she looked she saw trees bent by the wind. Even in summer Farraway could present a daunting aspect.

She listened at the door, wondering if Rorke was still there. Then she heard a window being opened somewhere below her own. Cautiously she looked into the corridor and this time found it empty. She went out, being careful to lock the door behind her and take the key.

There was no sign of Rorke as she went down, but she could hear movements at the back of the house. She tried the front door but it was locked. So were the three other doors that gave onto the hall, but a sudden inspiration made Sara try her bedroom key in them. The first two didn't budge, but the third one opened into a dining room. Quickly she darted back to the kitchen. To her relief the flares were still in place, far back under the bottom shelf of the pantry. She took them out and slipped some matches into her pocket. She'd never have a better chance to escape than this.

Everything was quiet as she crept into the dining room and turned the key in the lock behind her. Rorke would find all the doors locked, and it might be some time before he realized there was no one on the other side. In a moment she'd climbed over the windowsill and began to run.

The wind tore at her as she headed over the grass in the direction of the promontory. As she ran, she prayed. Let Jimmy Orken be on the watch. Let her stay free long enough to meet him on the beach so that he didn't run afoul of Rorke.

Soon her legs were growing heavy, but she was sure she could make it if only he hadn't discovered her gone. She stopped for breath and looked behind her, and her heart crashed painfully against her ribs.

Rorke was pursuing her with long, powerful strides.

She could have wept with despair. She had a head start of nearly three hundred yards, but she knew he could close that. Yet there might still be a chance if she could get to the promontory first and send up even one flare. She began to run again.

At last she dared to glance back again and discovered that Rorke had narrowed the gap to fifty yards. She knew there was no way she could escape him, yet something drove her onward. She could see her goal up ahead. The land was climbing sharply and the higher she went the more the gale tore at her. No place

on Farraway was free of the wind, but here it was a
fiendish enemy seeking to whirl her in a dance that
would take her over the edge. She could have screamed
with the pain in her lungs, but she had no breath to do
anything but force one aching leg in front of the other.
She could hear Rorke behind her. He was calling her
name into the gale. She threw all her efforts into a last
despairing attempt to keep ahead of him, even though
she knew it was useless. His voice came to her more
clearly, *"Sara, . . . don't."* She thought there was a
frantic note in his cry, but she couldn't stop to think
now. She drove herself on the last few yards and was
almost there when she felt his hand.

He stretched out, touching her but not managing to
catch hold, and in eluding him she lost her balance.
She stumbled, not to the ground, but seemingly into
the arms of the wind that tried to whisk her toward the
drop. Desperately she threw herself flat, slithering,
grasping frantically for tufts of grass that came away
in her hands, and the next moment her head was over
the side and she was staring three hundred feet down
at the rocks that had killed Laurel Calvin.

The world spun around her. She screamed but her
voice seemed to vanish into the blast. The only sound
that reached her was a desperate roar of Rorke's voice
from somewhere behind her, filled with the horror of
a nightmare come true.

Something was stopping her from falling. It was as
if a steel bar was clamped across the small of her back,
but her head still hung sickeningly in the void.

"Sara, give me your hand."

She managed to force one arm behind her and felt
her wrist seized. Then she felt his grip tighten as he
hauled her back.

He didn't risk standing up again, but rolled over with her until they were well clear of the edge. Sara lay still, her eyes closed, exhausted and despairing. Gradually she became aware that he was still holding her. Her face was pressed against his chest, which rose and fell sharply. She tried to force herself to be calm but the dreadful sight of those rocks remained behind her eyelids, making shudders go through her. Rorke tightened his arms around her. "It's all right," he said harshly.

Warmth began to steal over her. Terror was giving way to a sensation of blessed security. She felt as if nothing could harm her as long as those arms held her fast. Her shudders became slower, less violent. When she opened her eyes she found Rorke's face close to hers, his eyes filled with shock.

He released her and she had to suppress an instinctive move to hold onto him. He crawled back to the edge and hurled the flares over. When he returned, his face was pale and set and he moved like a man in a dream. He sat motionless beside Sara, his hands clasped between his knees, watching her, his chest heaving.

She stared back, trying to assemble her disordered thoughts. She'd gambled and lost, but she'd also discovered something. She knew now that Rorke hadn't killed his wife. She'd heard it in his voice, full of agony as he saw history almost repeated, and cried out a despairing protest. She'd felt it in the frantic hands hauling her back from the edge, denying the rocks their second victim. She was still dizzy, and the world spun around her. In that terrifying whirl she saw only his face, his eyes fixed on her with horror and bewilderment.

"Are you insane to come up here in this weather?" he grated. He passed a hand over his eyes and she saw that he was shaking.

"I had to," she managed to get out between gasps. "I told you, I don't accept that I'm your prisoner. I'll escape you any way I can."

"But you *can't*," he snapped. "For pity's sake, be sensible. You'd be dead on those rocks now if I hadn't been here."

"If you hadn't been here I wouldn't have gotten so near the edge at all," she flung back. "Who's fault would it have been if I'd gone down?"

His face became deathly pale, and she knew she'd struck a blow where he had no defenses. Strangely the knowledge that she'd hurt her enemy brought her no satisfaction, only a bitter ache.

When Rorke spoke at last his voice was flat and lifeless, as though every word was an effort. "When you're ready we'll get back."

She forced herself into a sitting position. Rorke got to his feet first and put out a hand to help her up. He'd have kept hold of her arm but she freed herself and walked clear of him, although her legs felt like jelly. "Let me help you," he said angrily.

"I can manage," she told him. It was bad enough to have failed, without having to take his arm for the journey back to captivity.

"When do you give up?" he groaned.

"I don't."

After a few steps she knew it had been a mistake to walk so soon. She'd run nearly two miles, much of it upward, and her whole body was complaining at this new burden before it had rested. But she gritted her teeth and forced herself on.

Halfway home Rorke took her arm and steered her firmly to a low rock. "You may not need a rest, but I do," he insisted. This time she yielded, glad of the chance to sit down.

"I should have known better than to leave you unguarded for a moment," he said, still gasping slightly. "Where did you hide those flares?"

"In the pantry," she gasped back, "at the very back, under the bottom shelf. You couldn't have seen them by accident. And there aren't any more, so don't waste your time looking."

He made a slight grimace. "I think I'll look just the same. You've got too many tricks up your sleeve for comfort. How did you come to have them?"

"Jimmy Orken gave them to me to send up when I'm ready to go. Now I've no way of signaling him," she added belligerently, "so you'll have to take me to the mainland in your boat."

"Do you think I will?"

"In the end, when Fergus doesn't come and you get bored with my company."

Rorke didn't answer in words, but he swept his gaze over her, taking in the curved hips and long, elegant legs. He brought it to rest on the valley between her breasts, and when Sara dropped her eyes she saw that their struggle had torn off the top two buttons of her shirt. The edges gaped, revealing the swell of her full breasts and the way they strained slightly against the lace that enclosed them. She hastily pulled the edges together. Disturbing memories flitted through her mind, the way they'd lain together on the cliff, the feel of his chest rising and falling against her, the warmth of his body.

She became aware that her heart was pounding again, and there was a new trembling in her limbs, but these seemed to have nothing to do with her exertions. They were somehow connected with the way Rorke was looking at her. The grimness had left his mouth and it relaxed into gentle lines, and his lips were slightly parted, allowing the ragged breath to come through. His dark eyes had lost their cold irony, and somewhere far back in their depths a fire was smoldering. "Sara..." he whispered, and hesitated. He took a painful breath, then continued, "We should get back before it starts to rain."

Heat was pulsing through her body. It seemed directly linked with the thundering of her heart, and was the most delicious sensation she'd ever known. But his words made it die abruptly, and now she realized how cold the wind had become. She shivered and wrapped her arms around herself. Rorke reached out as if to pull her against him, but he checked himself and spoke harshly. "We'd better hurry."

She walked the rest of the distance in a daze, trying to come to terms with the fact that Rorke had looked at her with naked desire, and she'd been shaken by the strength of her response. There'd been no time for thought, but now she forced her mind to shake free of the spell in which he seemed to hold it. She knew nothing about him. Her conviction on the clifftop that he was innocent of his wife's murder was probably no more than an aberration, caused by the fact that he'd just saved her life. From now on she'd have to be more on guard than ever.

Large drops of rain began to fall when they were in sight of the house and they hurried the rest of the way. "You'd better go up and change your clothes," Rorke told her when they were inside. "Where's the key to your room?"

"In there." Sara pointed to the door of the room through which she'd made her escape. "I locked it inside and left by the window. I'd better climb in and get it."

He stopped her. "Oh no! After you got in you'd close the window behind you and I'd have to spend tonight sleeping outside on the ground in case you escaped again. Stay here."

He went out and she heard him climbing in through the window. A moment later he opened the door into the hall. He accompanied her upstairs and unlocked her bedroom door, then turned and left her at once. Puzzled, Sara watched his retreating figure. She'd expected to be locked in again. It occurred to her that her efforts to hold the two edges of her shirt together had been wasted. Rorke hadn't even looked at her.

An ache had settled just behind her eyes. She rubbed them, hoping the pain would lessen. Instead it seemed to be spreading rapidly. Noise reverberated through her head, getting louder with every wave. She removed her shirt, moving gingerly, not to disturb her head too much, but when she went to a drawer for a sweater she had to lean over and a dead weight seemed to hit the top of her skull from the inside.

When she went downstairs a few minutes later she found Rorke piling logs into the burner. He glanced up when he heard her, and immediately straightened at the sight of her tense, pale face. "What is it?"

"Nothing, I've got a headache. I'll take something for it and it'll pass. It's probably all the excitement on an empty stomach," she ended with an attempt at flippancy.

She set down the pills she was carrying while she filled a tumbler of water. Rorke examined them and frowned. "You'll feel better when you've had something to eat," he agreed. "Sit down and I'll get it."

She let him. It was becoming hard to think through the pounding in her head, and she closed her eyes thankfully. When she opened them again Rorke had set some scrambled eggs and a mug of tea on the table before her. He watched while she toyed with the food, and asked, "It's a migraine, isn't it? Doctors don't prescribe what you're taking for ordinary headaches."

"I get them now and then," she muttered, speaking with difficulty.

"I wish..." He stopped himself as he saw her wince. "I'm sorry. You're not up to listening. You'd better get to bed."

She let him help her up the stairs. Cymbals clashed in her head, flashes of light danced before her eyes, and she was past caring about anything but the pain she had to contend with. In her room she managed to undress, crawl into bed, and lay her head down gingerly.

When she awoke, the pain had receded into a dull thud, and she was in total darkness. She tried to lift herself up in bed but suddenly Rorke was there, pressing her gently backward. "I'm here," he told her softly, and it didn't seem strange that he'd offered the words as comfort. "How is it?"

"Better than before," she whispered, "but I need to take some more pills."

There was the brief flare of a match, then the glow of the oil lamp. "Tell me where to find them."

"In that bureau, second drawer down."

He pulled the drawer open and rummaged. "There's only one left," he said at last.

"Isn't there another bottle?" she asked frantically.

After some searching he returned to the bed. "I can't find another bottle, Sara," he said gently. "Could you have put it somewhere else?"

"No," she said hopelessly. "This only happens two or three times a year. The last time was only a few weeks ago, so I must have forgotten to stock up, I thought I was safe for a while..."

She bit back a groan at the thought of the agony she'd have to endure, perhaps for days, with nothing to ease it. Rorke was leaning forward, peering at her, then abruptly he stood and left the room. He was back in a few minutes with a glass in one hand and the other holding something she couldn't see. He slipped an arm under her shoulders and lifted her gently.

"Take this." He held his hand close to her face so that she could see the capsule he was holding between his fingers. Sara took it and slipped it into her mouth. He pressed the glass to her lips and she swallowed mechanically.

"I always take two," she whispered.

"Not these," Rorke said. "I've given you something much stronger. One will do the trick, I promise." He pressed her gently back onto the bed. "I promise," he repeated. "Trust me, Sara."

The words echoed and reechoed through her head...*trust me*...*trust me*. Rorke stayed where he was, sitting on the edge of the bed. She watched him, drawn as if by hypnotism, and his voice seemed to come from a long way away. "Sara, can you hear me?"

"Yes," she whispered. Her head was full of echo chambers and his voice reached her several times over, but she forced herself to concentrate.

He leaned closer to her. "I want you to know something. I didn't murder my wife, and I don't mean you any harm. You can go to sleep safely. Do you understand that?"

She tried to say something but black waves of sleep were pulling her down into their depths, mercifully blotting out the pain. Rorke watched as her eyelids drooped and the lines of tension in her forehead eased. He took her hands in his and sat beside her for a long time.

Five

———

When Sara awoke, the pain was gone. She moved her head gingerly from side to side and found that all was well. Next she tried easing herself up into a sitting position. Again there were no ill effects, and she sat there, enjoying the blissful sensation of being well again.

The room had the dull light of afternoon. She wondered if it was still the same day, or the next day, or a week later. Her sleep had been so profound that she'd totally lost track of time. Before that her recollection was only of a haze of pain. She'd thought she heard Rorke telling her that he hadn't killed anyone, but she might have imagined it. She closed her eyes and pursued the memory, trying urgently to pin it down. Had he really said that, or had she dreamed it because she so much wanted it to be true?

Once again she could hear him asking for her trust. Her mind was still confused, but her body had begun to relax from that moment. It was disconcerting to know that she, who'd always relied on her own strength and control, had relinquished herself into the hands of a man logic told her she should be wary of.

She threw off her nightgown and headed for the bathroom. A shower might make her feel more like the cool, efficient Sara Tancred that she was accustomed to.

She yelped at the first shock of the cold water, but after that it was delicious to feel the sleep being washed away. She shampooed her hair, rubbing vigorously and enjoying herself until it got into her eyes.

"Damn," she muttered, as it dawned on her that she had no idea which way she was facing. She identified the wall and began to grope around, but then she suddenly found the towel placed in her outstretched hand.

She dried her eyes quickly and looked, but she was alone. Only the bathroom door, standing slightly ajar, betrayed that anyone else had been there.

The long wall mirror showed her a young woman whose fair skin had the bloom of youth and health. An athletic life had left her body slender and taut, but her shape was still softly feminine. Her breasts were high and generously rounded, with two rosy nipples that had peaked into telltale firmness as she thought of Rorke. The knowledge that he'd looked at her nakedness made a surge of response tremble through her. She was assailed with an overwhelming sense of how much she wanted this man to find her beautiful. She wanted that almost as much as she wanted to believe his innocence.

She hurriedly dried off. Her nightgown was in the other room so she wrapped the towel around herself, holding it in place with one hand because it was on the small side.

She found Rorke standing by the bedroom window with his back to her. He turned and she saw that his face was pale with strain. His shirt looked as if he'd slept in it, and was half undone, revealing the reddish brown hair that covered his chest. He flushed slightly when he saw her. "I heard your cry and I came in to see if you were all right," he said defensively.

"The cold water took me by surprise."

He came closer and put his hands on her shoulders, looking closely into her eyes for any sign of pain. "I'm all right now," she assured him.

"Thank heavens," he said fervently. His hands tightened in a sudden convulsive movement, pulling her forward against him so that his arms could enfold her. "I'm sorry, Sara," he murmured against her damp hair.

It was warm and sweet in his arms, and she felt again the sensation of safety she'd known when he held her on the cliff. She knew this must be another aberration and she should push him away, but when she lifted her hands it was only to draw him closer. "It wasn't your fault," she said.

"I think it was. You've been living on a knife edge these last few days. You've been frightened, but you'll go to hell and back before you'll admit it. You don't cry and you don't give in. You're not that kind of woman. But you're not as fully armored as you tried to make me think, and something had to go. I guess what happened on the cliff was the last straw. I tried

to tell you just before you went to sleep that you have
nothing to fear. I'm not sure you heard me."

She pulled away and looked up quickly into his face.
"You did say it? I didn't imagine that?"

"I'm not a killer, Sara," he insisted quietly.
"You've got to believe me."

Indescribable happiness was flooding through her.
She couldn't speak, but when Rorke looked down at
her he saw her feelings shining from her eyes. The
sight overwhelmed him, and he broke every stern rule
he'd made for himself and bent to kiss her.

The moment she felt his mouth on hers Sara knew
how much she'd wanted this. He kissed her gently at
first, moving his lips with slow, persuasive movements that urged her to open for him. Her lips parted,
allowing his tongue to slide between and explore the
soft inner flesh, and at once he tightened his embrace, taking possession of her more deeply.

His hand was pressed into the small of her back,
pressing her against him, and her mind began to form
an intimate picture of the body she could feel next to
hers. There wasn't an ounce of fat on that powerful
frame. His thighs were made of bone, muscle and
sinew, hard and unyielding, leading to firm narrow
hips; his stomach as flat as a board, and his great chest
rose and fell deeply with his breathing. The towel had
slipped down, enabling her to feel the rasping of his
hair against her skin. The sensation excited her and she
moaned, arching closer to him.

Rorke lowered his head to kiss the tender, sensitive
skin just below her ear. Sara shuddered as fire streaked
through her with every flickering movement of his
tongue. He tantalized her with devastating skill, fi-

nally coming to rest at the base of her throat. "Sara..." he said huskily.

Her only answer was a sigh. It inflamed him past bearing. He tugged at the towel and the next moment she was naked in his arms. Sara twisted against him eagerly as he began to run his hands over her, tracing the curves and valleys of her shape, rejoicing in her beauty. He lifted her swiftly in his arms and laid her on the bed. Even before he'd set her down he was once more moving his hands feverishly over her. He traced her breasts lovingly, teasing the nipples with subtly moving fingers, so that she moaned in agonized delight and arched toward him, seeking deeper, more intimate caresses.

She pulled at the remaining buttons of his shirt so that they fell open and she could run her hands over the whole expanse of his chest. His eyes blazed into hers as she reached lower and found the fastening of his jeans. She opened the zipper and felt him pressing hard and urgent against her palm. She gasped with pleasure, knowing he wanted her as much as she wanted him, and in a moment she'd know the fulfillment for which her whole body was yearning. "Rorke," she whispered longingly.

She felt a sudden jolt as if an electric charge had gone through him. The eyes so close to her own were opened wide in amazement. Then he seized her hands and abruptly forced her back, holding her away from him as he tried to regain control.

"Rorke," she said, bewildered.

"No," he grated. "Sara, this isn't right."

He drew back with a sharp movement and stared down at her, appalled as he took in her soft, swollen mouth and drugged, hazy eyes. "My God," he muttered thickly, "I said you could trust me, I never meant..." He bent to pick up the towel and covered her with it. His hands were shaking. "It's all right," he said harshly. "There's no need for this."

"Rorke—"

"I said it's all right," he declared with suppressed violence, and walked out before she could speak again.

Sara lay there, trying to force some calm into her throbbing flesh. It was difficult because in a few moments Rorke had roused her body to a pitch of almost unbearable desire. The mutual attraction that had tugged at them almost from the first had finally exploded into the open with devastating results. She'd reached for him, not only physically, but with an instinctive yearning of her whole being. She knew there was no going back from this moment, but Rorke hadn't yet faced that.

She dressed slowly and went downstairs. The storm was over but the wind still gusted wildly outside. The fire in the stove was blazing merrily and Sara knelt before it and shook out her hair to dry.

He came in a moment later, bearing more logs, which he dumped on the floor. His gaze flickered over her, but all he said was, "Don't get too close. You'll scorch yourself."

She spoke in a deliberately casual voice. "That pill you gave me must have been pretty strong. How did you happen to have them?"

"I have my own supply."

"You, too?" she asked with sympathy.

"Yes, I know a bit about holding things in and what it can do to you."

"How long did I sleep?"

"Twenty-four hours. I promised you one would do the trick."

"Yes, you said to trust you," she reminded him. "I'm glad I did."

Rorke didn't seem to hear this. He was putting things on the table. "You'd better come and eat something, Sara. You've been a long time without food."

"I do feel a bit light-headed," she agreed.

"I know you do, and it's dangerous. It makes the world look differently and you do silly things you wouldn't normally dream of," he said, concentrating on the table.

"Or it clears your mind and helps you to see the truth," she told him, looking at him steadily, willing him to look at her.

"Come and sit down," he ordered.

She went to the table and said no more while he served up the meal, starting with thick mushroom soup from one of his plentiful supply of cans. "You need to have something hot. The next course is cold salad," he explained.

Her eyes opened wide when she saw the salad. "How did you get fresh vegetables?" she asked in amazement.

"I have a vegetable patch outside. I don't live entirely on what I can get from the mainland."

"It's good," she told him, tasting it.

Behind the small talk another conversation was going on. He was trying not to meet her eyes, fearful of what he'd read in them, and even more afraid of what his own would reveal. But he revealed it anyway in the vibrant tone of his voice, the set of his head as he looked away from her, the strain that was apparent in every line of his tense body. And when he couldn't resist looking at her, she saw the desire that tormented him, and her eyes told him she wanted him, too. "Are you ready for some more tea?" he asked abruptly.

"Yes, please," she said demurely. She was playing a waiting game.

He poured the tea and followed the salad with bacon and eggs. "You've got everything you need now," he said. "I'm going back to work." He strode out, across the hall, and through a door on the far side.

Sara frowned, wondering what kind of work he did in that room. She'd assumed he'd meant his vegetable patch, or something to do with the house. She finished her meal, feeling the strength flow back into her, and followed him, opening the door with careful movements, and slipped quietly inside.

She found herself in a large room with high ceilings, lined with books. There were two very tall windows hung with brocade curtains that looked as if they'd seen better days. They looked onto a magnificent view of the starkly beautiful countryside, washed with the vivid colors of sunset.

Near the window stood a heavy desk with a leather chair. Rorke was sitting there, his head bent over something he was writing by the light of candles. He looked up and frowned at the sight of her. "Is there something you want?"

"Only to satisfy my curiosity," she said, closing the door and coming further into the room. "What kind of work do you do in here?"

"I write."

"You mean professionally?"

"Yes." The terse monosyllable was unencouraging.

"What kind of books?"

"Philosophy."

She regarded him quizzically. "Are you making fun of me?"

"No, why should you think so? Because I don't look like your idea of a philosopher? Would you believe me if I had white hair?"

He was right. This powerful, hypnotically attractive male should have been a lumberjack or a pirate. She thought of philosophy as a sedate occupation, and there was nothing sedate about Rorke's disturbing virility, or the pagan glint in his eyes. "You'd certainly look more the part with white hair," she confirmed. "I can't imagine you as a philosopher."

"That just shows you how dangerous it is to go by appearances," he remarked lightly. "At one time I held some very strong beliefs about the nature of good and evil. I included a long chapter about it in one of my books. The sales tripled when I was put on trial for murder. My publisher, poor fellow, was hoping for a guilty verdict. That would really have given him a bestseller."

"Is that what's known as 'being philosophical' about something?" asked Sara quietly.

"What do you mean?"

"I mean that indifferent voice you use to pretend you don't mind."

"I haven't minded about anything for the last eighteen months."

"That's not true."

"All right," he said heavily. "It's not true."

"You minded terribly about your wife," she continued, knowing she was venturing into dangerous territory. "And you still mind about her or you wouldn't be doing this."

"I have to do it. I owe her justice."

"It's more than justice. It's got something to do with the way you loved her. You couldn't live with her or without her. You told her so." She saw him stiffen as the significance of this reference dawned on him, and hurried on, "Fergus didn't translate that for me. I understood it myself."

"I might have known you'd be the one person in ten thousand who could read Latin," he observed wryly.

He came over to the fireplace and threw another log on. The flames blazed up, filling the room with shadows. The light outside was beginning to fade. Black clouds hovered, warning that the storm wasn't yet over, and the grass was almost flattened by the wind.

"Rorke," Sara said urgently, "tell me what happened. I don't just mean what you told the court, but everything, *please*."

He stood looking down into the fire. Even in this light she could see how he was racked with indecision. Once before he'd come close to telling her, but then retreated hastily. To tell this story he'd have to bare his very soul and trust her as he'd trusted no one else. Sara understood all this, and her heart nearly stopped, for nothing in her life had been so important to her as this moment.

"You told me she didn't love you as you loved her," she prompted him tentatively.

"That's true. When I married Laurel I was about as crazily in love as a man can be. But I knew she didn't love me, and probably never would. She married me

because she felt safe with me. She was terrified of
Fergus, and she wanted a man who could protect her
from him.

"Fergus's prosperity is largely an illusion. His affairs have been going badly for years. His father was
a Scottish industrialist who'd built up his own little
empire. His will divided his fortune between them.
Laurel got her inheritance in cash. Fergus got the
business. In a short time he'd brought it to its knees,
and started bullying money out of Laurel.

"She was unstable. I believe the medical term is
manic depressive, but I couldn't find out for sure because she wouldn't see a doctor. Fergus had made her
terrified of them. He kept saying she was only fit for
an asylum, and if she refused his demands for money
he'd threaten to have her certified. He was her only
relative. As her next of kin he could've taken charge
of her money.

"If he'd ever tried to have her certified I doubt he'd
have found it that easy, but he always threatened her
in her worst moments, when he could make her believe anything.

"After we married, I became her next of kin. She
chose me because I was big and ugly, and have enough
of a temper to give Fergus a fright. She made no secret of it.

"Sometimes she was quite normal, and then she was
the sweetest, most lovable person you ever knew."
Rorke's face was momentarily lit by a glow that had
nothing to do with the fire. Sara turned her head away
not to see it. "But suddenly she'd go into a black
depression that would last for weeks," he continued.
"It would end with a bout of frantic gaiety, then she'd
be normal again, but always a little more desperate as

she realized she was getting worse. She'd sob in my arms night after night, and make me promise that I'd never let her be 'put away.' She used to say she'd die first.

"Once I tried to force her to see a doctor. I thought he'd reassure her, and if she could get over her fear of treatment we could start a new life. I made an appointment and told her she had to keep it. I meant it for the best, but—" Rorke took a shuddering breath "—she tried to kill herself. I didn't dare do that again."

His voice faded suddenly, and for a moment Sara had a glimpse of the appalling loneliness of that marriage: the woman locked away inside herself with her endless fear—the man, passionate, generous, self-sacrificing, always giving what he'd never receive in return.

"After the wedding Fergus behaved himself for a while," Rorke resumed, "but then he started troubling her again. He got to her while I was away giving a lecture. She was in one of her depressions, susceptible to anything he said. I came home to find she'd taken an overdose of sleeping pills."

There was a silence. Rorke seemed to be struggling with some emotion that threatened to overwhelm him. Sara didn't dare speak. At last he continued, "When I was sure she was going to be all right I went after Fergus, and caught up with him in his office. I left him unconscious. The doctors diagnosed three cracked ribs and a broken nose."

"Yes, he mentioned that, although he gave a different reason. According to Fergus you were retaliating because he protested at your treatment of her, and he said she begged him not to press charges because she was afraid of you."

Rorke gave a crack of mirthless laughter. "He moved heaven and earth to stop any charges. He claimed it was for Laurel's sake, but the truth was he didn't want me talking in court about his need for money. Some of his creditors would have started to understand how bad things were.

"It was after that that Laurel and I came to live here. By then I was writing books full-time, which I could do anywhere. And on Farraway I could protect her better, or so I thought.

"I hoped she'd find some peace, she'd been so happy here as a child. And in a way that happened, but it took her even further from me. She began to retreat into her childhood. She'd felt safe with her father, and now I became a substitute for him. I didn't fight it because it seemed to make her contented. She insisted on sleeping in the room she'd had as a child. I slept in the room you have now, alone."

He hesitated. Sara held her breath, sensing that he was coming to the last barrier and the hardest, one that he might not be able to cross.

"One day," he said at last, speaking with great difficulty, "I had to go to the mainland. Laurel chose to stay here." Rorke's fingers were tightly clenched. "It was dark when I returned. I couldn't see her anywhere, but I found a letter she'd written to me. It was as though the darkness had swamped her mind. She accused me of marrying her for her money and then plotting to have her committed. She wrote that I'd been her last hope, and since I'd failed her, too, she couldn't face life any longer.

"While I was reading, Fergus appeared. He must have arrived in Glenrie secretly and waited until I was seen leaving Farraway, then come here, knowing he'd have her to himself. He told me that Laurel had finally 'seen through' me, and had decided to put herself back 'under her brother's protection.' Somehow he'd managed to make her more frightened of me than of himself. She must have promised to go with him, and told him to leave her alone while she got ready. All the time she meant to give him the slip and kill herself. She wrote the letter and left the house without Fergus seeing her.

"I pushed past him and tore out of the house to search for Laurel. There was a good moon that night, and eventually I saw her up on the promontory. She was standing, looking down at the rocks. She screamed when she saw me, and told me to keep away from her. She was demented with fear.

"I pleaded, swore that I hadn't betrayed her, but I couldn't get through to her. I reached out to take hold of her. I was going to pull her to safety, but she managed to wriggle away from me and...." Rorke dropped his head into his hands.

Sara felt as if something was choking her. She wanted to reach out and comfort Rorke, but she feared to intrude on such agony.

At last he continued, his voice hard and emotionless, as though it was only by deadening all feeling that he could bear to speak. "I went down to the rocks. It was low tide and I found her easily. She must have died immediately. I carried her back to the house, but there was no sign of Fergus. I soon found out why. The police came and I was arrested.

"He'd followed me out of the house and come far enough to see what happened on the clifftop. Then he hurried back to the mainland and told the police that he'd seen me murder my wife."

Sara stared at him, ghastly visions chasing themselves through her brain. She could see and hear everything, the man taking the fatal step forward, his hands outstretched, pleading, and then the sickening scream as the woman dropped three hundred feet to the rocks below.

She knew things he hadn't told her as well: how he must have flung himself to the ground, crying his wife's name aloud, straining to see down to the rocks, holding his breath, listening for the faint cry that would tell him she was alive and hearing only the desolate sound of the distant waves.

She imagined him clambering over the rocks until he found Laurel, and clutched the broken body to him, heard the despairing sobs that racked him, and about which he would tell no one on earth.

She thought of Fergus. How could that smiling, friendly man possibly be guilty of such wickedness? And yet she recalled the faint, cold watchfulness that had never left Fergus's eyes.

She'd seen the wedding picture through the tinted spectacles that Fergus had cunningly forced on her, but suppose she'd heard Rorke's story first? Wouldn't it have been obvious that the frightened look on Laurel's face as she gazed up at her husband meant not that she was afraid of him, but that she saw him as her last hope and feared that even he might not be enough to save her. And wasn't the menace on Rorke's face really intended as a warning to Fergus, just as the large

hand around his bride's tiny waist signified that she
was under his protection now?

"Didn't the letter make any difference?" she asked.

Rorke raised his head. "There was no letter, Sara,"
he said softly. "I hadn't thought to take it with me
when I left the house. All I could think of was finding
Laurel. Either Fergus took it then or he came back for
it before he left the island to get the police.

"God knows I wouldn't have wanted anyone to read
it normally, the way it blackened me. But at least it
stated plainly that she meant to take her own life. It
would have cleared me if it had ever been found. But
there was only my word that it had ever existed.

"Fergus spun a wonderful tale about his little sister, terrified of her brutal husband. He told how he'd
tried to intervene to save her and got assaulted for his
pains, and of course he had witnesses to the beating I
gave him.

"On my side I could produce nothing. Laurel's state
had been a well-kept secret. During her bad spells
she'd stayed away from people. Even friends who
knew she had 'funny moods' didn't see her enough to
appreciate that it was a serious long-term condition. I
coped with her suicide attempts alone because I knew
how she dreaded doctors. I never guessed that I was
storing up trouble for myself. But when it came to that
point there wasn't a shred of proof that she was unstable."

"What about the doctor you'd made an appointment with?" Sara asked. "You must have told him
something about her condition at the time."

"Yes, but he hadn't actually seen her, so he could
only tell the court what I'd told him. I might have been
imagining things, or trying to frighten her into going

mad, which was what the prosecuting lawyer suggested.

"Fergus claimed he'd come to Farraway because he was worried about Laurel, and wanted her to return with him. But while they were talking I arrived and started to threaten her. She ran away from me. I followed and murdered her by throwing her from the top of the cliff."

"But why?" Sara asked. "What could Fergus gain by pretending you'd murdered her?"

"A lot of money. Laurel's fortune was tied up under her father's will. A small amount went to Fergus immediately on her death. She was able to leave me the rest, but only for my lifetime. After that it would go to our children if we had any. Since there are no children, it would revert to Fergus after me. If I'd been found guilty of her murder I'd have been barred from inheriting and he'd have gotten the entire sum at once.

"I think he'd have done it even without the money motive. I humiliated him in front of his employees, remember. He'll hate me for that until the day he dies.

"I'm an Englishman, Sara. I didn't know there was a Not Proven verdict until my lawyer told me. At my trial I realized what a solid, reliable figure Fergus presented, and how unconvincing I sounded. The small inheritance he'd already received from Laurel had enabled him to paper over the cracks. So when I told the court that he'd been trying to extort money from her because of the perilous state of his affairs, no one believed me."

"But if he needs money so badly, why doesn't he just sell this island?"

"He can't. He only has possession for his lifetime. He can neither sell it nor raise money on it. Despite the sob story he fed you about his sentimental memories of Farraway, Sara, the fact is that Fergus cares nothing for this place. God knows how long I'd have had to wait for him to turn up here, if it wasn't for you. You're a godsend. Sooner or later he'll come for you. And when he does, I'll be waiting.''

Six

Sara felt as if she was waking from a dream. While Rorke spoke she'd been lost in the story he told, feeling every sorrow and anger with him. Now she was forced back to reality. She was still his prisoner, held by force on this island until she'd served his purpose. She shivered as she thought of that purpose and how it might end.

"Rorke, please give it up," she begged. "It won't work. You'll never get Fergus this way."

"Fergus murdered my wife as surely as though he'd pushed her off that cliff with his own hands, and he's walking around freely. I can't allow that. He has to pay for Laurel's death. I promised her that when I was in prison waiting for my trial, and I'll have no peace until I see him behind bars. I can't get to him in London, he's too well guarded. It has to be here."

"But a confession gained at gunpoint would be worthless," she said urgently. "The police wouldn't even look at it."

"But a private investigator would. The people Fergus Drummond has defrauded for years would be glad to get their hands on the details of his methods. I don't want a general confession. I want chapter and verse of every piece of fraudulent business he's ever indulged in—names, dates, Swiss bank account numbers, the lot. I can use that to get independent evidence that will stand up even when he retracts the confession. If I can show how close to bankruptcy he was when she died they'll see why he lied about me. At best I may clear my name. At worst I'll see him in jail for fraud, and that'll be better than nothing."

"But it won't be that simple. If you turn that gun on Fergus, even if it's only to frighten him, you're doing something very dangerous. Guns go off whether you mean them to or not. Suppose he holds out on you?"

"He won't, or not for long. Fergus isn't a brave man. That's why I've got a double-barreled shotgun. Just the sight of it will allow me to get what I want."

"And Fergus will immediately tell the police you threatened him with a gun. They'll believe him, because of the past, and you'll be the one in jail."

"I'll have to risk that."

"And the risk of being a murderer? Will you take that risk, too?" she demanded passionately. "You're trying to clear your name, but you could end up doing the very thing you've been accused of."

"I know what I'm doing with a gun."

"Perhaps you do, normally, but you're not in a normal state. You're at the end of your tether, aren't you?"

"Yes," he said tersely. "And that's why I'm not giving up. This is all I have left."

She came to stand beside him near the fire, looking up into his partly shadowed face. "And what about me?" she asked deliberately.

"What can I say to you except that I'm sorry? It isn't fair to involve you, but I have no choice. It'll be over soon, and then you can go home and forget everything."

She gave him a little shake. "Stop fooling yourself," she urged. "You know neither of us is going to forget anything that's happened between us." When he didn't answer she put her hand against his cheek. A tremor went through him at her touch and for a moment she thought he'd reach for her. But he gently drew her hand away.

"No," he said unsteadily, "I won't forget you, Sara. But I also won't do you any more harm than I have already."

"I'm not light-headed any more," she told him. "I can see things clearly, and the truth is still the truth. You know what the truth is about us, don't you, Rorke?"

"Sara, stop this," he said harshly. "You don't realize what you're saying."

"Are you telling me I'm imagining it?"

"No, you're not imagining anything. I know the truth, too, but I also know there are some truths that mustn't be faced."

"Is that the philosopher talking?" she challenged him. "It doesn't make any sense to me."

"Then I'll spell it out. You're vulnerable. You're my prisoner—"

"I'm not trying to bribe the jailer if that's what you're implying," she interrupted him.

"I know that. I know you mean it but...look, when people are in our situation, it sometimes happens that...they get involved. I'm your captor. That gives me the power, and a prisoner sometimes imagines..." He came to a halt.

"Oh, give me patience!" Sara exclaimed, half in amusement and half in anger. She appealed to an invisible audience. "Now he's lecturing me about captive psychology! Do you think I'm so feeble that I've started to 'imagine' things after less than a week?"

"No, you're not feeble, Sara. You're one of the strongest women I've ever known, and I admire you. That's why I've confided so much to you. But things will look differently when you're away from Farraway."

"And when will that be?"

"I don't know."

"Are you going to be so strong-willed all the time?"

"I can try," he said raggedly.

"Rorke, what's happened to you? When we came back from the cliff, the way you looked at me—"

"That was different," he interrupted her harshly. "Things have changed."

"How?" she asked, bewildered.

He ran a hand through his hair as he sought for a way to answer her without letting her suspect how she was wringing his heart. When they returned from the cliff he'd still thought of her as the confident woman who challenged him to madness. He'd seen only her courage. Since then he'd discovered the price she was paying for that brave exterior, and she'd never look the same to him again.

He thought of how her naked body had felt in his arms this morning, and the memory sent a wave of heat surging through him. But it was superseded at once by the picture of her face as it had been at that moment, pale in the aftermath of pain, and without the veneer of sophistication. With her hair falling wet around her face she'd looked suddenly very young and vulnerable, and he'd pulled back, appalled at what he'd been about to do.

Now she stood before him in the flickering firelight, offering him the prize he'd yearned for through fevered nights and tormented days. Her hair had the slight fluffiness of recent washing, and the fire's glow turned it into a golden aureole around her face. He could see the flames reflected in her eyes. She was like a flame herself, he thought, red-gold, elusive, burning any man who dared to come too near. Her face was turned to his in passionate appeal, and for a moment aching desire threatened his resolutions, and he nearly pulled her into his arms.

He mastered the impulse and he took a step back, half turning away from her. "Things have changed," he repeated. "I've had time to think."

"Time to decide which truths you're brave enough to face, and which ones you're not," she demanded ironically.

His eyes blazed at her. "There's one truth you ought to be frightened of, Sara, though it doesn't seem to have occurred to you. You're alone with a man who hasn't had a woman for eighteen months. Sure you look good to me. You look *very* good, a banquet after starvation, but is that all you want?"

In the silence that followed he saw the pain that flickered over her face, and he ground his fingernails into his palm. "That isn't true," she whispered at last.

"Isn't it? Would you care to take a chance on that?" She flinched but made no reply as he continued coldly, "It's better if we don't forget that we're still adversaries, Sara. I respect your right to try to escape, but I'll still stop you. Nothing has changed between us."

It was a lie and he knew it, but he was desperate. He watched her with haggard eyes as she walked from the room, her head high. He'd been cruel to be kind. His resistance was at a low ebb, and she'd have won this battle if he hadn't ended it quickly. So he'd flung an insult at her pride and knew it had defeated her. But he hated himself for it.

Sara was looking down onto the rocks. They reared up to her, their sharp teeth turning into fingers to claw her into their savage embrace. She gasped and shook herself awake.

She'd come to bed early to get away from Rorke, but she'd found that sleep was worse than lying awake. Her dreams were haunted by the rocks. She'd awoken, then dozed off again into a nightmarish half sleep in which reality was horribly distorted. It had been a relief to shake off the nightmare and this time she meant to stay awake.

She got out of bed and went to splash some cold water on her face. The night stretched ahead of her with nothing to occupy her thoughts but the dread of sleeping again. She wished she could read something, but she had no light and no book. She paced the floor for a while until at last she came to rest on the window seat and stared out over the countryside, looking anxiously for any sign of dawn.

She could still hear Rorke saying coolly that nothing had changed between them. He'd underlined it by locking her in again tonight. Bleakly she wondered if he was right. Was her own response to him no more than the emotion of the prisoner adjusting to captivity? Everything in her denied it. Her armor of self-reliance and detachment had been in place a long time, but the hunger she'd seen in this man's eyes had cracked it. He needed warmth and love, and the sweetness of laughter to bring him back to the world he'd rejected because it had rejected him. And his need had reached out to her, touching her heart to a depth that no man had ever plumbed before.

It hadn't occurred to her that the feeling might not be mutual. She knew she'd won Rorke's respect. He'd proved that by confiding in her, and surely that made her more than just a prisoner? But then she remembered the shining look on his face as he spoke of Laurel, the wife he'd loved despite everything, for whose sake he was doing this. Laurel had been dead for eighteen months, but Rorke's feelings were still bound up in her, and his desire for another woman was merely a matter of practical circumstances. The thought of how she'd thrown herself at a man who regarded her as nothing but "a banquet after starvation," made her drop her head in her hands and groan aloud.

Almost at once there was a knock on her door. "Sara," Rorke called from the other side.

"Yes," she called back hastily.

"Are you all right?"

"I'm fine."

Rorke unlocked the door and came in. He was wearing pajamas. "Are you ill again?" he said when he saw her by the window.

"No, I'm fine," she insisted, wishing he'd go away.

He came further into the room. "I heard you groan. Is your head hurting you?"

"My head's all right. Don't tell me you were sleeping outside my door again."

"I couldn't sleep. I went down for a book and when I came up I heard you pacing. Couldn't you sleep, either?"

"It's not that. I prefer to be awake."

He nodded. "Nightmares?"

He was standing between her and the bed, preventing her from climbing back in and covering herself. She was directly in the light of the moon, knowing that her short nightgown didn't cover her adequately. To shield herself with her hands would be to admit that his words earlier that evening had hit home, and her pride prevented that.

"Do you want to talk?" he asked.

"No thank you. What would be the point?"

"I'm good at talking dreams away. It used to help Laurel."

"But I'm not Laurel," she said with bitter jealousy. "And I'm not in the least like her. I don't need comforting and looking after—"

"Don't you?" he interrupted quietly.

She jumped up from the window seat and began to walk around, trying to get out of the revealing moonlight. "I've been looking after myself for years," she said firmly. "You're just another problem to be coped with. We're adversaries, remember, and fraternization with the enemy is dangerous."

"Yes, I know," he agreed. But he stood there and made no attempt to go. "Sara..." She paused and looked at him. What she saw in his eyes made her grow very still and hold her breath. "I didn't mean what I said," he said quietly. "Not a word."

She didn't answer, except that her tense immobility conveyed a message that he understood. His gaze was fixed on her face. She was in shadow but he could just see that her defensive mask was back again and he couldn't bear it. She'd invited him into her warmth, and he'd rejected her, turning back to the chill isolation where he'd lived so long, only to discover that it was home no longer. He didn't know what he'd find in her, but she'd destroyed his old refuge, leaving him no place to go but her arms.

"I didn't mean it," he repeated huskily. "You have to believe me, Sara." She moved closer to him, looking up warily into his face. The scent of her sweet freshness invaded him, making his senses ache. "I said anything I thought would stop you," he told her desperately. "You're so vulnerable, I couldn't ta—" he stopped, embarrassed at the old-fashioned phrase.

The wary look vanished. A gentle smile broke over her face and she touched his cheek. Her eyes were alight with something he didn't recognize, it was so long since he'd seen it. "You couldn't 'take advantage of me'," she teased softly. "Oh, how Victorian."

He could feel her fingers easing gently behind his head, drawing it downward. It was becoming hard to think, but he forced the words out because it was important that she should know. "I meant to carry it through," he murmured, "but I guess I'm not as strong as I thought." The last word was muffled against her mouth.

Their kiss was long and deep, beginning in tenderness and growing in urgency as their mutual passion asserted itself. He tightened his arms until Sara was crushed against him, and she felt the urgency in his whole body as it strained against hers. Her lips opened and he invaded her at once, roaming his tongue over the soft inside of her mouth, seeking the places where he knew he could make her quiver with delight. It was only a few hours ago he'd first held her naked flesh in his arms and discovered the force of her desire for him. Then he'd fought his passion down. Now he knew he was free to unleash the storm that possessed him, and he trembled at the thought of what was to come for them both.

She seemed to weigh almost nothing as he picked her up and placed her on the bed. He was shaken by the feeling of how slight she was against his big frame, and for a moment he could do nothing but sit there, holding her against him.

Sara sensed his fear and indecision and moved quickly to pull open the buttons of his pajama top. In a moment she'd removed it, and there was no restraint in her hands now. She caressed him in sensuous discovery, following the swell of muscles beneath the warm skin, the ripple against her palms. She traced the line of his neck, his spine, feeling the shudders that shook him as her soft fingertips found one sensitive spot after another.

A wave of happiness swept over her. Now she was free to love him, free to explore the secrets of this magnificent male body, to which her own responded so mysteriously, and with such intensity. Beneath his tough exterior the passionately loving, generous man he'd once been was still alive. She wanted that man and she'd fight to find him, and win his love.

At first he let her make love to him, as though he hardly dared believe what was happening. Then he seemed to come to life, stripping the nightgown from her in one movement. She remembered that Rorke had lived in enforced austerity for eighteen months, and knew she was playing with fire. But she wasn't afraid of fire. A woman with less reckless courage would have balked at the task of changing his mind, but she refused to allow herself to think of the odds against her. The consequences of possible failure were too terrible to contemplate.

So she put everything she had into the seduction of Rorke Calvin—her heart, her lips, her willing body— because she was trying to make him remember the sweetness of life before he took a risk that might shut him off from it irrevocably.

He was tracing the outline of her curves with his fingertips, lingering over the swell of her breast, a hip, running luxuriously down the length of her slender flanks, then back up to the junction of her legs, the valley of her waist and toward her throat, where he caressed the bare flesh before beginning the descent again. He explored her like a man who'd forgotten what female beauty looked like, and for a moment the words, "a banquet after starvation," came back to haunt her. But she dismissed them. There was something in Rorke's eyes that was almost reverence, which told her she wasn't just any woman. She was the woman who'd roused in him a desire that all the striving of his conscience hadn't been able to suppress.

He urgently claimed her breast in his open palm. The delight was agonizing as he gently teased the nipple. Her skin seemed to warm and flower under his touch, crying out for his intimate caresses as though it had been made for him alone.

His lips were bruising hers, making her moan deep in her throat. The sound seemed to inflame him because he began to trace a path of fire around the soft inside of her mouth. His tongue was a weapon, not caressing but assaulting the delicate skin, driving her to madness with its harsh, flickering forays. When he released her she was gasping.

He took her lower lip between his teeth, teasing it gently, sending little shock waves tingling through her flesh, tantalizing her until her breath came in a mind-less sigh.

He drew away for a moment, but only to feast his eyes on her nakedness. Moonlight flooded into the room, outlining every detail of her eager, expectant body, revealing her swollen breasts with the peaked nipples. He moved his hand to her waist, the fingers splayed out over the swell of her hip. "You're incredibly beautiful, Sara," he said huskily. "No man should trust a woman who looks like you. It would have been safer if I had kept you at arm's length."

He loomed over her. She took his face in her hands and whispered up at him, "It's too late to say that."

In the shadows she could just make out his mocking smile. "I thought you believed it was never too late to turn back."

"It's too late for us," she whispered. "It was always too late."

Her voice grew husky as Rorke slid his hand over the silky skin of her stomach, flexing his fingers slightly as he went. Each movement sent stabs of pleasure into the depths of her loins, and instinctively she arched against him, inviting deeper exploration.

At once he rose and discarded his pajama trousers. Then he dropped quickly beside her, lowering his head to take one peaked nipple between his lips. The flickering jabs of his tongue challenged it again and again, while waves of sensation washed over her at the sweet torture.

Her innermost self had lived protected by a moat, which no man, even those she'd thought she loved, had been able to bridge. Rorke Calvin hadn't bridged the moat: he'd made it vanish. With his first touch her heart had found the way home. Now she felt the caution of years melt like ice vanishing beneath the sun. The trickle became a stream, then a river, then she was being swept headlong into a whirlpool taking her faster and faster toward the center of desire.

Heat surged through her loins and out to the furthest reaches of her body. The tender skin of her inner thighs was burning for him. She felt his manhood, taut and hard against her, warning her that the moment had come. Now he slid easily between her legs, claiming the heart of her passion with one urgent movement. She gasped at the sensation, poignant in its sweet intensity. It felt wonderfully right and natural to have him there, filling her with himself, thrusting slowly, deeply into her.

Her hips seemed to move of their own accord, rocking back and forth to meet and withdraw from him, claiming and releasing him, but never letting him leave her entirely. Sara hadn't thought of herself as a passionate woman, but now she discovered she'd been wrong. All this time she'd secretly known things, things that every woman knew deep within her, but

which only the right man could draw forth. A cry of
physical release broke from her, and she was shaken
by convulsions as the pleasure mounted to heights that
were almost unbearable.

Only as her head cleared, and she saw Rorke's desperate face above her, did she realize that she was
weeping, she didn't know why.

"Don't—" he pleaded in a voice she'd never heard
him use before. "Sara—" He began to kiss her face
gently where it was wet. Starting with her eyes, he
moved down slowly to her mouth. His tongue traced
the outline of her bruised lips with tender, caressing
movements, inviting her to open to him, until at last
she did so with a sigh that was almost inaudible. He
heard it however, and trembled.

Now there was time to enjoy the warmth stealing
over her as he coaxed her response with hands and lips
and loins, until she was helpless to do anything but
yield to her desire. She was still languorous from their
first union, but his touch excited her as easily as if they
were making love for the first time, and now she found
he was carrying her to new heights. Nothing in her life
had prepared her for the breathless intensity of passion that surged through her. She'd longed for their
mating, but she discovered she hadn't fully understood what she'd wanted. This agony of raw pleasure,
this blind, compelling need to satisfy a physical crav-
ing, shattered her with its force. She no longer recognized herself. Cool, self-reliant Sara Tancred had
vanished and been replaced by a woman who was only
complete when she was united with this one man.

There was breathless delight in that moment, and
heart-stopping awe at what followed. He made love to
her now with gentleness and patience, drawing out

every long, piercing movement until she was half demented with ecstasy and frustration.

When she could endure it no longer, she clasped him tightly, raking his back. His movements became faster, more powerful as he carried her over the edge into the abyss of blinding sensation. They fell together, spinning downward, dizzily at first, then more slowly, and finally coming to rest in a safe place where she discovered that his arms had held her all the time.

As she fell a cry began in her heart and burst from her throat, mingling with his own. She thought she heard him call her name, but the sound was gone before she could be certain.

Seven

Sara awoke the next morning to a sensation of bliss. She felt heavy and sated, as though the memory of fulfillment still glowed in her limbs. Her body was newly alive in every place where Rorke had touched it, and he'd touched it everywhere. Her flesh had been branded with those intimate caresses, so that even the thought of them could send heat coursing through her now. Sometimes he'd been fiercely demanding, compelling her response, sometimes he'd enticed her gently to passion. But always his touch had inflamed her.

She'd have loved to see his face, but the darkness had shielded it, except for the glint in his eyes. She knew only the feel of the warm flesh, and the power of the body that had claimed and possessed hers. Now she felt as if she'd awoken to find the world presented to her on a platter, freshly washed and polished, the colors gleaming.

Rorke was still asleep, lying on his back. The sheet had been flung aside and there was nothing to hide the magnificence of his great, naked frame. She longed to run her fingers across his chest, following the hair down to his flat stomach, but she didn't dare wake him. For the first time, she realized, she had him at a disadvantage, and could study him without his knowledge.

Evey line of his body was taut and firm. It was the body of a man who lived hard—muscular but lean. Looking at his long thighs, with their swell of steely muscles beneath the skin, Sara wondered how she could ever have tried to outrun him.

She propped herself up on one elbow and studied his face. It looked younger and less harsh with the lines smoothed out by sleep. Now his eyes were closed she could no longer see the expression of wariness he'd so often turned on her, and she wondered how he'd look when they opened next. Would the memory of the passion they'd shared the night before be in them?

His face was unusually gentle, the relaxed mouth showing the sensuous curve that nature had given it. He'd looked like this in the past, Sara thought, before grief and bitterness had wounded him. This was the face his wife must have seen, but when those dark eyes had opened to her they'd been full of love. The thought gave Sara a pang.

He was a dangerous, tormented man, desperately in need of help, yet bristling defensively at anyone who came too near his pain. But now she'd started to understand him. Even while she was still unsure what to believe about Rorke, his unhappiness had touched her heart. Now she knew he was innocent, the floodgates had opened and a tide of desire had come sweeping through and engulfed her. She could make him hers. All she needed was the chance.

If Rorke had opened his eyes at that moment he'd have seen Sara's chin set in a firm line that betokened the onset of an attack of stubbornness. Her mulelike obstinacy had been her friend in other critical situations, but never one like this. She was used to getting what she wanted, and what she wanted now was Rorke Calvin's heart and mind. She wanted him free of his ghosts, free to love her and accept her love.

He'd chosen a dangerous path because there was nothing in the world he feared to lose. Sara knew she had to make him love and want her so desperately that he'd refuse to do the thing that might separate them. She had to make the dead hand of Laurel Calvin release him. It was as simple and as difficult as that.

Rorke stirred and she moved away at once, knowing he wouldn't want to wake and find her watching him. She slipped out of bed and stretched before going to the window and throwing it wide. It was a glorious day, with the morning sun casting a dazzling light over the harshly beautiful landscape. Sara took a deep breath, rejoicing in the feel of the fresh air on her naked skin.

Then she saw it!

The sight caught at her throat and she leaned dangerously far out of the window, trying to keep it in view. High up in the pure blue of the sky a golden eagle swooped and wheeled. Even from here Sara could make out the size of the seven foot wingspan, held rigid as the great bird soared without effort on the wind currents. Her heart almost stopped with the beauty of it, and she risked leaning out another inch.

"What the hell are you trying to do?"

Before she could answer Sara felt Rorke grab her by the waist and yank her back into the room. "Does nothing stop you?" demanded Rorke, holding her firmly against him.

"Oh, don't be silly!" she said impatiently. "If I'd been trying to escape I could have walked out of the bedroom door, couldn't I?" She pointed to where it stood slightly ajar, as he'd left it last night. Rorke drew in his breath at the sight.

"Then what were you trying to do?" he demanded, not letting her go.

"I'd just caught sight of a golden eagle." Sara twisted in his arms and managed to look out of the window again. "It's gone now," she said crossly. "Why did you have to disturb me? I wanted to see where it was headed."

"Why?"

"Because," she explained, exasperated, "though you seem to have forgotten it, I'm here to photograph eagles. I ought to be out there with my cameras this minute, not wasting my time here."

He seemed to become aware of her naked body pressed against his. Looking down, Sara saw that her nipples were peaked and rosy, telling an embarrassingly frank tale. Another moment and she knew that their sensual communication was perfect. The sudden hard swell against the top of her thigh confirmed it. She began to draw him close, moving her fingers caressingly against him, but he pushed her away abruptly.

"Of course, let's not waste your time," he said curtly.

"Rorke, I didn't mean—"

"Let's get out there," he interrupted, turning away to the door.

"Are you saying that I can leave the house?" she asked, not sure she'd heard him correctly.

"*We* will leave the house."

He strode out of the room. Sara groaned at the mischance that had made her say those words at the wrong time. She plunged under the shower, taking it as cold as possible in an attempt to calm the tumult in her blood that he'd roused so easily. By the time she stepped out she had her feelings under some sort of control, although she wasn't sure how that control could stand up to a day spent close to him.

But then her professional side asserted itself. She was here to take photographs, and this might be her only chance.

She went downstairs dressed in her oldest jeans and shirt. On her feet she wore strong boots for climbing, and over her shoulder she'd slung a leather jacket. Her blond, bouncy hair was severely repressed by a scarf. This was her working outfit.

She found Rorke busy serving up a hearty breakfast. His manner was efficient and detached, as if the scene earlier had never taken place. When they'd finished eating he produced a small picnic basket and crammed it with sandwiches while she prepared for her day's work.

She pulled open her camera case, setting film aside, checking cameras, lenses, filters. As her fingers performed the familiar efficient actions, her mind fell into line with them. She was being taken over by the other Sara, a professional doing the thing at which she was an expert. This other Sara could push personal considerations aside, and feel only the combination of calm and anticipatory excitement with which she always approached a job.

When she'd locked the case, Rorke lifted it. "I'll take that," Sara said, making a gesture for him to put it down.

"It's heavy as blazes," he objected.

"Of course it is. There's a lot of equipment in there. I'm used to carrying it. What do you think I do when you're not here?"

"And I'm supposed to carry the picnic basket while you stagger along with that?"

"I'm grateful for the chivalry, but it's quite unnecessary. I've carried that case through far worse conditions than we're going to meet today. Can we go now? I want to catch the best of this light."

Without another word he picked up the camera case and walked to the front door. On second thoughts, she decided, if he wanted to haul that heavy weight around, let him. She'd have more energy for doing her job.

After they'd trekked a couple of miles she knew she'd made the right decision. The ground was becoming increasingly stony and uneven, and the landscape grew harsher and more withered. This part of the island faced north and almost nothing seemed to grow here. The few bushes and shrubs that tried had a defeated appearance, and the grass was more brown than green. As the land climbed she was glad of her heavy boots. Despite the sun, the wind was up again and it buffeted them unceasingly as they made their way upward.

"We'd better have a break here," Rorke suggested. "The next stage is rock climbing, and you'll need some energy."

As they sat down and Sara began to rummage in the case Rorke indicated the huge crag up ahead, and asked, "Think you can face that?"

"If it's the only way to get the pictures, I'll face it," she confirmed.

She pulled out a camera, swiftly fitting on a huge telephoto lens. Over her shoulder she slung a shoulder rest into which she put the camera. "You can't climb with that thing over your shoulder," Rorke objected.

"Don't worry, I won't try. Before we start again I'll pack it away."

"Then why bother to get it out? There's nothing in the sky."

"But there might be at any moment. If I waited until something appeared before I got my equipment out it would be gone before I was ready. Ninety percent of wildlife photography is lying in wait. It's rather like being a hunter."

At that moment she saw a black shape above her. It soared on the air currents in magnificent disdain. At once she forgot Rorke, forgot everything but the tantalizing chance held out to her for a few brief seconds. Through the telephoto lens she could just make out how the feathers on the great wings separated at the tips, giving the impression of long fingers. But at this distance no other details were clear, and although she was reasonably pleased with the shots she took, it was obvious that she'd have to get a lot nearer.

"All right," she said, packing her things away. "I'm ready when you are. Let's see how close we can get."

She followed him to where the rocks started in earnest. To her relief she didn't have to climb a rock face, but merely to make her way over boulders. But the boulders were large and steep, and as the ground fell away beneath them she grew increasingly reluctant to look down. Once the stone under her feet wobbled ominously, but Rorke, who was ahead of her, yanked her swiftly onward to where she could just make out the eagles' aerie, up ahead.

"This is as close as you can get," he told her.

"Surely not. It's not even on the same clump of rocks that we're standing on. Why didn't we go up the other one? We'd be nearer."

"There's no way up that one. It's almost sheer. The only way across is too dangerous to contemplate."

"Let me see it."

Sighing, he led her forward a few more yards, and she saw what he meant. They were standing near the top of a thick tower of rock that stood almost parallel to another tower. The only way across was by a kind of natural stone bridge made of two protruding rocks that reached to within a foot of each other. It was just possible for someone who had a good head for heights. Sara didn't, but she immediately declared, "I want to go across. I'll get some marvelous shots over there. Where we are now is too far away for even my strongest telephoto lens to get close-up."

"Sara, will you be sensible? You can get perfectly good shots from here."

"That's for me to judge," she said firmly. "Anything I could take from here would be only second best, and I didn't get my reputation by settling for second best. If you won't help me across I'll go alone."

He looked at her closely for another moment. "All right," he said at last. "We'll go."

It was only when they got really close that Sara realized just how tricky it was. The protruding rocks were L-shaped, with the short sides forming a narrow floor. The long sides made walls, but long exposure to the wind had blasted them smooth and there was nothing to cling to.

Rorke went first, edging his way along the ledge, his back to the drop, leaning as close against the wall as he could. After every step he leaned cautiously down and pulled the camera case along a few inches. Sara held her breath as he eased it across the gap and went on a few yards to where the rocks broadened out. After a moment he returned and took the picnic basket that Sara was cautiously pushing toward the gap. When he'd deposited this safely he stretched out a hand for her.

Sara stepped forward tentatively, wishing it was possible not to look down, but if she was to place her feet carefully it couldn't be avoided. Taking a deep breath she began to edge forward, trying not to be too aware of the uneven rock beneath her feet, or the gap with its sickening vision of stones two hundred feet below.

"Take my hand," Rorke advised.

Ice seemed to come over her limbs. She couldn't have moved if her life had depended on it. The drop that yawned below seemed to hypnotize her and was beginning to spin.

"*Sara!* Don't look down. Look at the rock and move when I tell you to. Move your foot to the right, a little further, now put it down. Don't look . . . trust me. Now the other foot. You're over."

She moved sideways, inch-by-inch, feeling the ledge widen beneath her feet. Rorke tightened his grip and

he began pulling her faster until they reached the safe
place where he'd dumped the baggage, and pulled her
forcefully into his arms. "Why didn't you listen to
me?" he demanded. "I warned you how it would be.
We could both have gone down."

"Sorry," she gasped.

"Little wretch! You aren't sorry at all! You
wouldn't care what happened to me as long as you got
to your damned eagles. You'd better rest here awhile."

"No, I want to start working right away. We're not
too far from the nest and the light's good now."

Rorke stared at her, and his eyes held the same look
they'd held once before when she'd first defied him.
But he said nothing.

To her delight Sara found that she was now higher
than the aerie, with an uninterrupted view. The distance was far enough for her not to alarm the birds,
yet close enough for her powerful lenses to work.

There were two eagles, each with the distinctive dark
brown plumage, with golden brown on the head and
nape, and thickly feathered legs. One was about three
feet long, and the other a little larger. Sara knew this
was probably the female.

For two hours she worked intently. Almost as
though they realized they were required to pose, the
birds took off and landed, wheeled and swooped.
Then the male departed, leaving the female standing
on the crag, presenting a perfect profile of the sharp
head, glittering eyes and overhanging beak. Sara used
up a whole roll of film on her as she perched there,
grasping the rock with her talons, attentively waiting
for her mate's return. As she finished the roll Sara
looked around anxiously. "There's no sign of him,"
Rorke said, reading her thoughts. "I'll keep my eyes

open while you change the film. You've only got three rolls left, by the way.''

"It'll be enough," Sara said, hurriedly completing her task. "If that male comes back soon I'll have all I need."

Almost on cue the male reappeared, silhouetted against the sun. Sara risked a shot with the sun shining straight into the lens, knowing it would be a winner if it came out well. Then, as the eagle shifted position, she saw that he had a large object in his beak.

"It's a rabbit," Rorke said, following her gaze. "He's been hunting."

The bird started his descent toward the nest with the rabbit held between pitiless talons. The wings began to fold. Feathered legs extended, it came lower and lower, touching down with exquisite grace and precision. Sara caught every detail, leaning out at a perilous angle, only half aware of Rorke's fingers curled around the waistband of her jeans to keep her safe. "Wonderful!" she breathed. "I got everything. That'll make a fabulous set." She began loading another roll.

"If you've got everything why are you loading up again?" he demanded. "No, don't tell me . . . just in case."

"That's right."

He disengaged his fingers and flexed them painfully. "Can we have something to eat now?"

They began to unpack the basket. To her amazement Sara found a bottle of champagne. "We kept the cellar stocked when we lived here," Rorke said in answer to her look. "There's still some down there. But I have a feeling we should save our celebration for after the climb down."

Sara sighed, but realized he was right.

"Do you always go to these lengths?" Rorke asked after he'd assuaged his hunger.

"If I have to. You don't get decent wildlife shots unless you're prepared to do things that are dangerous and uncomfortable."

"But you're terrified of heights, and not just because of what happened the other day. You are anyway."

"Yes, but if I let things like that stop me I wouldn't have had a career," she pointed out. "When I'm climbing I'm a bit like the man who kept banging his head against a wall, because it was so nice when he stopped. When I get down again I always want to yell, 'I did it'."

She cried the last words aloud and the eagles rose up sharply, shrieking their indignation. Rorke promptly rescued her sandwich as she dived for the camera and began to click madly at the two birds. They wheeled directly above her and she rolled onto her back, shooting upward into the light so that the eagles appeared as menacing silhouettes. When the last shot was taken she set the camera down but stayed where she was. "Did you see them?" she demanded exultantly. "Rorke, did you see that?"

"Calm down," he urged, touching her gently.

But he could tell that she hardly heard him. Sara was on a "high" that had nothing to do with the altitude. This was the reckless exhilaration of achievement, the most potent drug in the world, and while she was in its grip, he realized, she was scarcely aware that he existed. He leaned down, blotting out her view of the birds. He had one glimpse of her face, half laughing, half crying, before he tightened his arms around her. Then he was kissing her angrily, commanding her to return from a world where she seemed to be happy without him.

"Sara...Sara..." he said, trying to call her back.

Her eyes met his, the eyes of a dreamer coming down to earth. He bent his head again to kiss her jealously while the wind tore at them and the eagles screamed their fury overhead.

"If it wasn't freezing cold up here I'd have every stitch off you," he growled. She smiled up at him provocatively. *"Sara..."* He forced himself out of her arms, knowing he was on the verge of doing something that would have been wildly dangerous on that high ledge.

Sara sat up and began to pack away her equipment, trying to keep her hands steady. Her heart was thumping excitedly, and all her sensations were heightened. The air around them was as clear and sparkling as the champagne that awaited them.

They finished their meal without further disturbance. Sara surveyed the breathtaking panorama before her. From here they could see almost all the island and the glinting sea beyond. "I couldn't have managed it without you," she said. "How did you know where to bring me?"

"I've always loved to watch the eagles. There's something about their freedom that makes me marvel. I think I've forgotten what it feels like to be so free. They were hunted down until they were almost extinct. Now they have to come to this remote place because it's only here that they can feel safe. I've come here for much the same reason."

He looked up into the sky where the male eagle was once more soaring loftily on the air currents as though they were there solely for his pleasure. The movement threw Rorke's face into profile and Sara saw again the slight hook of the nose that made him so like an eagle. It also reminded her that she was still in his power. "The light's fading," she said. "We should be getting home."

She dreaded the journey back. On the way up, driven on by the need to reach her goal, it had been possible to force herself across the abyss. But now, with her pictures safely tucked away, there was less impetus to give her artificial courage. The sun had passed behind heavy clouds and a gray light covered the land.

When they reached the gap, Rorke went across first as he'd done before. Then he came back for her. "Don't look down," he commanded, stretching out his hands. "Just keep your eyes on me."

The wind gusted bitterly past her cheeks. Her eyes smarted and the knowledge of what lay below her made her head swim and the nausea rise in her stomach. But there were Rorke's hands reaching steadily toward her, and his eyes that held her gaze hypnotically.

Then, somehow, the abyss had passed away beneath her and was gone. It was all over and Rorke's arms held her safe. She clung to him and he tightened his embrace, holding her still until she was ready to move. "You mad woman," he whispered in her ear. "You stupid, crazy female! Are you listening to me?"

"Mmm!" she said contentedly against him, and didn't see the tender look he gave her.

Eight

It was almost dark by the time they got back to the house, and they hurried the last few yards. Nothing was said when they reached the kitchen but they went into action as a team, motivated by the same thought, to get warm and comfortable as soon as possible. Sara lit the candles and the oil lamps, then put the kettle on. Rorke hauled some logs in from the yard and piled them into the woodburning stove. Sara had never needed to use it, but Rorke said it was larger than the gas stove, and therefore better suited for what he had in mind.

He took a flashlight and led Sara out to a small brick shed in the yard. It was drafty inside and the flashlight illuminated hunks of meat hanging from the ceiling. They gave off a pungent odor. She held the flashlight while Rorke took down some meat and carried it back to the house.

"It's venison," he explained when he'd laid it on the table. "I shot a red deer just before you arrived. It has to hang for a fortnight before it's ready to be cooked."

"A fortnight?" Sara echoed. "Is that why it smells like that?"

He grinned at the sight of her face. "No, that's the pepper I've been brushing it with every day to preserve it. Don't worry, it won't kill you. I'm a better cook than you are, not that that's saying much."

She aimed a swipe at him. He grinned and pointed at the kettle. "Get on with the tea, woman. Make yourself useful."

It was almost the same command that he'd given her on their first day, but now it was different. Tonight everything was colored by a glow of irrational joy that radiated from inside her. It was irrational because her situation was full of danger and uncertainty. Rorke was still keeping her prisoner, and was intent as ever on confronting Fergus with a gun. The future might yet be as dark as her nightmare the previous night.

But the sharp edge of her fears was blunted by the delight of this man's nearness. As long as she was with him she felt safe from the hostile world that threatened them. She wanted nothing better than to be here alone with Rorke, exchanging the silly domestic jokes of intimacy. She wanted to forget the freezing night outside the window. Above all she wanted to forget how precarious was her happiness, how soon it might all be snatched from her.

The fire in the stove was beginning to crackle and heat filled the kitchen. She watched Rorke as he stood there, drinking deeply of the hot tea she'd made. The lamps cast a soft tawny light over him, and as he began to thaw out every line of his body suggested contentment. Almost unthinkingly he reached for her and drew her against his side. She snuggled against him, feeling the warmth seep through to her bones, wanting to say to him, *Don't you see how good it is to be like this—how happy we can be? How can you risk losing it all?*

She tried to convey this to him by taking one of his hands in hers and rubbing the last of the chill away, all the time aware that he was looking at her with a question in his eyes.

Suddenly he removed his hand from hers and cupped her chin, still holding her with his other arm. He dropped his head and covered her mouth in a gentle kiss. In other embraces he'd been driven by anger or passion that was half rage. But this soft laying of his lips on her own was rich with the promise of tenderness and her heart almost stopped beating.

She tentatively slid her arm around his neck, fearful of breaking the spell. She twined her fingers in his thick hair, caressing him, loving him with heartaching intensity, trying to tell him that she belonged to him and would be desolate without him.

At last he drew away, and there was something in his eyes that she'd never seen before. He took her hands in his and held them for a moment before releasing them. "We have work to do," he said unsteadily.

"Yes," she agreed, smiling at him. She knew how to be patient. "What do you want me to do?"

He was watching her mouth and it was a moment before he spoke. When he did he shaped the words with the effortful intensity of a man forcing himself to concentrate. "There's some lard in the pantry. We have to rub it over the venison."

When the meat was saturated with fat and garnished with herbs from Rorke's vegetable patch, they set it in the oven. In a short time the kitchen was filled with a savory fragrance that made Sara's head swim. It seemed a long time since they'd eaten on the crag. "When?" she asked longingly.

"There's still a lot to be done. How about peeling some potatoes?"

While she got to work he vanished into the cellar, reappearing a few minutes later with a bottle of claret.

They ate in the kitchen for warmth, but Sara found the best china and glasses and set the pine table in fine style. When she'd finished it looked ready for a feast.

It was her first taste of venison, and she thought she'd gone to heaven. The day's exertions had left her famished and Rorke watched her in amusement as she cleared her plate. "You're worn out," he said, filling her glass with claret. "If I'd known the tricks you were going to pull I'd never have agreed to that trip."

She shrugged. "It's my job. Wildlife is always found in awkward places. What happened today was par for the course. Anyway, it's better than working in a grocery store."

"Is that what you did before?"

"I had to. I wanted to go to university, but my mother had died and my father made me leave school to look after him. A friend of his owned a small grocery store and my father got him to give me a part-time job. Dad wanted to rule my life for his own convenience, and sticking me in a dead-end job meant he could keep control of me, or so he thought." Remembered anger tinged her voice.

"And you actually allowed yourself to be bullied like that?" Rorke queried, one eyebrow raised. "You meekly obeyed your father's orders? *You?*"

"I was sixteen," she said defensively.

He sighed in apparent relief. "I knew there had to be an explanation."

"All right, funny man! I was sixteen and there was nobody to fight for me. So at first I gave in, but it didn't take me long to learn how to fight for myself."

"What did you do?"

"He got a plateful of his dinner in his lap."

"If your cooking then was anything like it is now," Rorke said, grinning, "it probably did him more good out than in."

She laughed. "Well it wasn't the greatest meal ever cooked, but I took an awful lot of trouble over it. It actually came out quite well, for me. But then he wouldn't come and eat it. When he *did* arrive it had grown cold and he had the nerve to complain. I was furious. I knocked the plate off the table and said if he wouldn't eat it he could wear it."

"That sounds more like the Sara I know," he said appreciatively. "What puzzles me is how *I've* escaped this fate for so long."

"I caught my father off guard. I wouldn't give much for my chances of surprising you."

He poured some more wine into his own glass, not looking at her. "You gave me a few surprises today, Sara. I never thought you'd really go across that gap. You were terrified, but you're so mule-headed that you went on anyway. That's real courage, and I have to admire you."

To her astonishment she felt herself blushing with pleasure. She'd had other compliments but never one that disconcerted her like this. She hoped the candles on the table didn't give enough light for it to show.

"It's not courage," she said, playing with her fork. "It's just another kind of fear. You can do anything if *not* doing it frightens you more than doing it." Rorke looked at her questioningly and she continued, "Once I went to Africa to photograph some lions. I lived in a tent, and on my first night there I heard something. It was outside the tent, just by my head, and it sounded like an animal scratching around. My hair began to stand on end.

"I was certain it was a lion looking for his supper and I knew I couldn't bear to lie there all night waiting for it to strike. I was terrified of going out, but far more scared of just lying there for hours. So I crept out of the tent and eased my way around the corner to confront this fearsome beast."

"And?"

"It was a chicken!" she finished simply.

Rorke's crack of laughter seemed to hit the ceiling. He leaned back in his chair and shook with it. Sara laughed with him, delighted at the marvelous change taking place before her eyes. Helpless in the grip of merriment, he was a different man. He reached over and drew her to him for a kiss that held neither passion nor tenderness. It was a salute of camaraderie, of gratitude for a story well told and a satisfying end. Still laughing, he picked up his glass and raised it to her. She saluted him back, her eyes shining with the message her lips longed to speak.

There's this, too, my love. Laughter and wine and good fellowship... will you turn your back on them?

"I see what you meant this afternoon about not settling for second best," he commented when he'd calmed down. "You've clearly worked hard for it. What kind of reputation do you have, Sara? I never heard of you, but I've been out of circulation for a while."

"My name isn't heard in philosophical circles, but I'm reasonably well-known among people who commission wildlife photography," she said. "As a matter of fact, a national magazine did a piece about me a few weeks back saying..." she stopped suddenly.

"Saying what?"

"Never mind. It's not important." She'd suddenly realized that this particular tribute was exactly the kind to revive Rorke's suspicions.

"I'd like to know," Rorke persisted. Then, as she still hesitated, he added shrewdly, "Suppose I promise to take it in the right spirit?"

"All right. It said I'd go anywhere and do anything for a picture. I know you've always suspected that I slept with Fergus to get his permission to come here but—"

"No you didn't," he interrupted her. "I haven't believed that for days, and now I've seen what going anywhere and doing anything means as far as you're concerned. You're unstoppable. If Fergus had refused you his permission you wouldn't have slept with him. You'd have hired a boat and come across to Farraway on your own."

"You must be clairvoyant," she told him in amazement. "The idea had crossed my mind."

"I should have known the truth the first night when I saw the amount of baggage you'd lugged up here by yourself. I saw you from the window, carrying two bags, putting them down, going back for the other one. I ought to have realized then that a lady with that kind of determination and self-reliance wasn't...well, what I thought you were. But I've been out of human contact for a long time, Sara. I feel more like a wild beast than a man. I've been crazy with hate for so long that I guess I don't judge human beings very well. Try to forgive me for that."

She felt as though music was playing in the air around her, for he was saying everything she longed to hear. The passionate generous man he'd once been was still there.

"But there's something else," Rorke continued. "When I told you how Laurel died you believed me at once, without question, and you're the only person who's ever done that. It would be pretty shabby of me not to give you the same trust."

Her breath came out slowly in a long sigh of disappointment. She'd hoped for so much more. Until now it hadn't occurred to her to think it strange that she'd accepted Rorke's word without question. There was no outside evidence to show that he was telling the truth. But she'd believed the evidence of her heart, the only kind that counted.

She loved this man. She belonged to him body and soul, though he didn't know it, and wasn't ready to hear it from her. It therefore followed that it was impossible for him to have murdered an innocent woman. Such evidence might not stand up in a court of law, but to Sara the logic was irrefutable. "Rorke, let's get away from here," she pleaded with sudden urgency. "There's no point in staying now."

"There is for me. Fergus will turn up because he can't afford to sit and wait for anyone else to arrive. If there's a lot of commotion about you, the police will come nosing around Farraway again. He'll do anything to avoid that. You've been here long enough for him to start getting alarmed. He should arrive any day now."

Sara stared into her wineglass, hoping with all her heart that Rorke was wrong. She needed all the time she could get if she was to win him to her point of view. His words made it plain that she was still far from succeeding.

For a moment she was seized by freezing fear, as though she'd turned a corner and found herself confronted by a wall of black ice. If she failed, the future was a dreadful vacuum. Then she looked up and saw Rorke looking at her. She smiled at him, pushing her fear aside. This man was worth fighting for.

"I'm rather surprised that no one has come looking for you before this," Rorke said. "The one thing that could have spoiled my plans is if your family or friends started a hunt independently of Fergus."

Sara ran her mind over the people she knew and realized how unlikely that was. She'd dashed up to Farraway without telling her agent or her publisher where she was going because she expected to be back quickly. Liz had seen her leave the party with Fergus, but she'd been about to go abroad on vacation and would be out of touch by now. Sara's absences were too common for anyone to worry.

"Are you really so much alone, Sara?" Rorke asked gently.

"I hadn't really thought about it, but I suppose I am. I have no brothers or sisters, and my father only contacts me when he wants money. I've always been a loner by choice. Sometimes I've been in a remote place and thought, 'At this moment no one in the whole world knows exactly where I am,' and in a funny way I've enjoyed that.

"When I come home I've got friends I can visit anytime, but they're not deep friendships, because I'm away too much to nurture them."

"And you haven't got a husband. I know that, because I know you'd be faithful to him. Have you ever been married?"

"No. I was engaged once. I was just getting successful with wildlife photography, and he wanted me to give it up and settle for polite studio work and wedding pictures. He once told me, 'I'm not marrying you to spend my life seeing you off at airports'."

"So, faced with giving him up or giving up the job, you gave up him. Did you ever think of making the other choice?"

"No," she said slowly. "Now that I think of it, I didn't. I must have known instinctively that I could face loneliness, but I couldn't face being tied down."

"After your horrible father, it's no wonder."

"My father?" she mused, with a little frown into the distance as if she was examining the idea.

"It seems obvious to me. Because of him you see only domestic ties, not domestic joys."

"Yes, I suppose I do," she said, her voice filled with discovery. "I must be very stupid not to have seen it before."

"No, you're not stupid. You'd have seen it fast enough if you'd ever analyzed it, but I don't think you're an analytical person. You see only what you've got in your sights, and you go for it without looking to the right or the left."

"That sounds like me," she admitted with a little laugh, but immediately added defensively, "and what's wrong with that? If I wasn't single-minded I wouldn't have gotten anywhere.''

''There's nothing wrong with it, Sara, but it's dangerous to you. You don't see the tripwires that are so obvious to other people. You may be a loner, but you need someone to look after you, and do that kind of thinking ahead for you.''

Someone like you, she thought, but all she said was, ''It's not an easy job to combine with marriage.''

''Or with love?'' Rorke prompted.

She hesitated, then said, ''There was someone more recently, named Peter. He's marrying someone else now. He said he got tired of never coming first.''

''Well a man likes to come first in a woman's life,'' Rorke said gently. ''It's a trait of ours. You, on the other hand, are so terrified of losing your freedom that I imagine you lure men on with one hand and ward them off with the other.''

She laughed awkwardly. It was disconcerting to be with someone who understood her better than she understood herself. As Rorke had said, she wasn't analytical by nature, so it hadn't occurred to her that she'd been unconsciously sabotaging her own relationships when they began to look like a threat to her precious independence.

Only one man had made her want to belong to him, body and soul, and he was the one who'd taken her captive here. Yet perhaps it wasn't so strange. Rorke had imprisoned her body, but his understanding of her nature showed that he was no threat to her true freedom. She promised herself that one day she'd discuss this paradox with him.

Rorke was continuing, ''I'm afraid a woman who makes it clear to a man that other things matter as much as he does, or even more, comes in for a lot of abuse.''

''Oh, I got that all right,'' she agreed. ''He said I was becoming hard, caring for nothing except money and success. But it wasn't that at all. It was the excitement, the...'' She groped for words.

''The thrill of the hunt, the triumph when you've stalked your quarry to its lair and come back with a bigger and better trophy than anyone else,'' Rorke finished with a grin.

''That's exactly it,'' she said excitedly.

''It became pretty clear when I saw you hunting today. I'll bet you always get what you set your heart on, don't you? That ferocious determination of yours never lets up.''

She wondered why he apparently didn't see what she'd set her heart on this time. The eagle's prey had turned on him and now he was the quarry. But perhaps it was just as well. The bigger the game, the greater the need to track it undercover, and catch it unawares.

''I'm surprised at you, Sara,'' Rorke said unexpectedly.

''Why?''

''For letting yourself be troubled by the opinion of a fool.''

''It doesn't trouble me...well, yes, perhaps a little. No woman likes to be called hard.''

''But she doesn't have to believe it. You're a strong woman, but that doesn't mean you're hard. That Peter of yours was a fool if he didn't look behind the shell and see what's really there.''

''I'm not sure I know what's really there.''

"But I know," he said softly. "I know you're fierce and gentle, lovable and maddening, unchanging and unpredictable, candid and cunning, stubborn and persuadable, brave as a lion and nervous as a cat. I've learned all that in a few days."

"And yet all we've ever done is fight," she reminded him.

"Fighting with someone can be a very good way of getting to know them. Although we've only had a little time together I know you better than your damned Peter, who knew nothing at all. I'd have liked to discover all the rest of you. And I'd have liked to have the other times, too, when we weren't fighting but just..." She smiled at him. "I was just going to say talking, you shameless hussy," he growled. "I could have spent all my life getting to know you, and I'd never have reached the end of your awkward, infuriating, marvelous spirit."

"You say 'could have' as though it's impossible," she said lightly. "But nothing's impossible if we want it enough."

"But there are other things I want, too, and I have to put them first. I'm still a half-convicted man."

"What does that matter if I know the truth?" she asked earnestly.

"It matters to me. If I manage to clear my name... well, maybe I will. But until I do I've nothing to offer a woman."

"Nothing except yourself."

"But I'm like you, Sara. I don't know what 'myself' is anymore. I used to know who I was, but that was before I became filled with hate and bitterness. Now I look inside myself and what I see frightens me.

There's a darkness there that I can't ask a woman to share.''

The pain, which had been briefly banished from his eyes during this wonderful day, was there again. It hurt her to see it and she took his face between her hands, kissing him gently, possessively, on the mouth. "I'm not afraid of the dark," she told him huskily.

He took her hand in his and drew his lips across the palm. His breath burned her, and the touch of his mouth sent fire flickering through her. She curled her fingers slightly so that they caressed his cheek, and she felt the tremor that shook him. He looked up and Sara saw the naked longing on his face. She drew a long slow breath at the erotic promise in that look.

Then it was gone. He was expressionless, as if he'd drawn down a blind. He snatched his hand away from her and rose from the table. "I'll make the coffee," he said abruptly.

Nine

While Rorke made the coffee, Sara piled the dishes into the sink, wondering about the sudden unease that seemed to have come over him. "I'll wash up tomorrow," she said. "I'm too tired now."

"Yes, do that," he said over his shoulder.

He might simply have been concentrating on the coffee, but she had an odd feeling that he'd resisted turning to look at her. She stared at his back, her brow furrowed.

Her thoughts raced ahead to the night to come, and anticipation stirred in her loins. She watched his movements with eyes sharpened by desire, the sudden tautness of shoulder muscles against his shirt when he turned his body, the deft, long-fingered hands that last night had caressed her to madness, and tonight....

"Come and get it," he said, spooning powdered milk into the cups. "Then it's time for bed. I'm ready to drop."

There was a briskness about his voice that hadn't been there before. If she'd had any doubts they were settled now. He was shying away from her.

They drank the coffee standing up. Then Rorke went around putting out the lights until only one candle was left. In the great dark house it made a very tiny light, and Sara tucked her hand into the crook of his arm, walking carefully beside him as they climbed the stairs.

When they reached the bedroom Rorke went to the candle by the window and lit it from the one in his hand. "We don't need two, do we?" she asked.

"Sara, I'm sleeping in my own room tonight." He saw her turn astonished eyes on him and hurried on, "What happened last night...it was wrong for both of us. We only have a little time together. If we get too close we'll only..." He paused in exasperation. "Sara, I said then that I should have kept you at arm's length."

"You also said that you couldn't," she reminded him.

"Well tonight I can, and I'm going to, for both our sakes," he said, his voice shaking with suppressed feeling beneath the apparent calm.

Sara also spoke calmly. A listener would have detected no more than ironic amusement in her voice. There was no trace of her dismay or the fearful thunder of her heart. "Of course you can, Rorke. That's easy, isn't it? I mean, you had a woman last night, so tonight you can manage without one."

"Sara," she heard the danger in his voice.

"And let's face it, one woman's pretty much like another to a man who's been starved for eighteen months."

Suddenly he slammed down the candle. In the flickering shadows Sara could just make out the intense glint in his eyes. "Is that what you think, that you were just any woman?"

"You as good as told me once that that's all I was. 'A banquet after starvation' was how you—"

"I also told you I didn't mean that."

"Yes, you did, and I believed you, but what am I supposed to think now? You took what you wanted, didn't you, Rorke? I was just a little taste of something you'd been missing. But now—"

She never saw the movement as he reached out of the darkness and took her by the shoulders. There was the shock of collision as her body was forced against his, and held there by bands of steel while her words were cut off by bruising lips. She sensed the anger throbbing through him, felt it in the crushing pressure of his mouth, the ruthless imprisonment of her body in his arms, and the growl that vibrated through his flesh and then her own.

The dizzying narrowness of her victory made her almost faint with relief. Then that feeling was swept away by the turmoil of her sensations. Rorke's hands were on her clothes, tearing at buttons and fastenings, stripping her with feverish haste. She felt the cool air on her arms and shoulders as her shirt disappeared and he exposed her breasts to questing fingers.

She attacked his clothes with the same urgency. His buttons slipped away beneath her fingers and then the hair on his chest was rasping against her palms. She had only a moment to enjoy the sensation before he picked her up and tossed her onto the bed, looming over her and continuing to remove her clothes in purposeful fashion.

He unzipped her jeans in one quick movement. Then he curled his fingers around her waistband and began to draw jeans, tights and panties down over her hips in one smooth motion. In a moment she was completely naked, her clothes hurled out of sight into a dark corner. His own clothes followed them, and he dropped onto the bed beside her, pulling her fiercely into his arms. "You should have left the tiger sleeping, Sara," he growled. "But you insisted on waking him, so now you'll ride him to the end of the line."

"Not a tiger, an eagle... *my* eagle," she said huskily, hardly getting the words out before her mouth was smothered again.

He kissed her harshly, venting his rage at what she was doing to him on the sensitive flesh of her lips. He'd tried to prevent this happening and he knew she'd overcome his will with a child's trick. But knowing didn't help. He was in her net now and his struggles would merely enmesh him deeper. He'd stripped her clothes off meaning to teach her a lesson, but the lesson they were both learning was that he was helpless in the grip of his desire for her.

His tongue found its place inside her mouth where it seemed to belong. Her own tongue was challenging it, challenging *him*, goading him with his own desire until he did her bidding. She was laughing at him, knowing that the harder he tried to subdue her the more he was playing her game, showing him how insignificant his strength was when set against her weakness.

He felt her soft arms around him, their fragile hold unbreakable. Her slender body was lost beneath his, yet he was burningly aware of every inch of her. She seemed inspired, knowing the movements that would inflame him. His touch was ungentle with the raw urgency of his need, but she wasn't afraid to incite him still further.

She had a thousand caresses that he'd never dreamed of. Her fingers were full of witchery, tracing teasing lines on his skin that excited him unbearably. She tempted him with her hands and hips and finally imprisoned him, letting him feel the devastating sensation of her silky inner thighs gliding against him as she curved her legs around his hips. A groan was torn from the depths of him as she lured him into herself, possessing him at the moment he possessed her. She moved against him insistently, making fierce tremors go through him, and finally provoking him to an explosion that left him drained.

He felt a dreadful emptiness as he left her. He tried to tell himself that it was the inevitable aftermath of exhausting passion, but this was like nothing he'd ever known before. It was as though part of him only existed when it was united with her. Separate he was incomplete. He tried to dismiss the thought as fanciful, but the impulse to ask her if she felt the same was so strong that he had to bite his lip to remain silent.

He found he was lying with his head between her breasts. She was caressing his hair with gentle movements of her fingers. He looked up and saw that her face bore a smile of deep contentment. "What would you have done if you couldn't have gotten me to lose my temper?" he growled ironically.

"There was never any danger of that," she said, still with that mysterious smile.

No, he thought, there was no danger that he wouldn't react as she'd planned. On one level they might have just met, but on another their perfect harmony went back to the beginning of time. Even now he could feel his body singing to her tune, which made it all the more difficult to cope with another feeling, unfamiliar and totally irrational, that had taken possession of him this evening. "Did you ever seduce your damned Peter like that?" he growled.

"Peter?" she sounded genuinely puzzled. "What's he got to do with anything? Why did you think of him?"

"I've been thinking of him ever since you mentioned him."

She moved so that he was forced to sit up and look at her. "You became strange suddenly tonight," she said, "was that what was troubling you?"

"He seemed to be important to you."

"Not for his own sake. I think I remember him most because he gave me a view at myself that I didn't like. I wasn't really in love with him. At any rate, I'm not now."

She'd forgotten Peter so completely that she'd failed to detect the emotion that had inspired Rorke's strange behavior. In any other man she'd have seen it at once, but this one seemed so complete in himself, so armored in his assurance, that it had never occurred to her that he might be troubled by jealousy. If she'd dared, she'd have laughed aloud with happiness to think she'd made a chink in that armor through which she could creep and find him.

She wished she could see Rorke's face, but whether by accident or design his head was turned away from her. Suddenly he jumped off the bed, said, "Wait here," and vanished, taking one of the candles with him. A few minutes later he returned with two glasses and the bottle of champagne from the afternoon. Sara's eyes shone at the thought of an impromptu picnic, and she leaned back contentedly, propped against the pillows while Rorke filled her glass.

A sudden gust of wind outside made a window swing loose, banging madly against the wall. Rorke went and secured all the windows. Then he closed the door, not forgetting to lock it. As he returned to the bed he caught Sara's eyes on him, their expression wry. He matched it with one of his own. They were still adversaries, although passionate ones, and Rorke couldn't forget that fact.

Sara tried to thrust the thought aside. Rorke had shut out the rest of creation and now the world consisted of only the two of them in the near darkness, lit by flickering candlelight and the silver glow of the moon. Nothing existed beyond this room, this man, this love.

I'll remember tonight all the days of my life, she thought. But how would she remember it? As the night she'd bound the man she loved to her with chains that he couldn't break, or as the beginning of her defeat? And again there was the little chill of fear in her heart as she thought of the nightmare that might be drawing near.

She turned her head and found Rorke's eyes on her. He was drinking in the sight of her naked body sprawled against the pillows. She was relaxed in the languorous afterglow of passion fulfilled, but at the

look in his eyes she felt her skin become newly sensitive and grow heated. She lay quite still as he moved
his eyes lazily over her, lingering over details, her tiny
waist, the womanly curve of her hip, the full breasts
whose nipples were already beginning to grow taut
again as desire was reborn.

She made a move toward him but he prevented her,
taking her wineglass from her hand and pushing her
gently back against the pillows. "No, stay where you
are," he whispered. "You're so beautiful, I just want
to look at you. I didn't know anything could be this
lovely."

She lay still, watching his face, offering him all of
herself, letting the beauty of her body speak for her.
The silent communion of their flesh was more eloquent than a thousand words.

As if hypnotized, he reached out a hand and
touched the base of her throat. The little pulse that
betrayed her arousal was throbbing gently and he let
his fingertips lie against it for a long moment before
drawing his hand away and down over the soft swell
of her breast, lingering there.

There was a strange look on his face. She suddenly
recalled her own sensations earlier that day when she'd
first seen the eagle soaring into the heavens. She'd
known an incredulous wonder that anything on earth
could be so heart-stoppingly beautiful. Now she saw
that same thought mirrored on Rorke's features as he
beheld her.

"You're perfect," he murmured slowly, "utterly
perfect. I didn't see it before." He smiled faintly. "I
haven't spent much time standing back and looking,
but now...you might have been created as a blue-
print for how a woman ought to be. Eve must have

looked like you, a perfect creation to tempt Adam
until he was half out of his mind.''

''Philosopher,'' she teased him softly.

Her thoughts were becoming blurred as his fingers
traced lazy circles on her skin. She gave herself up to
the rapturous sensation that was gathering strength
inside her. It mounted slowly, giving her time to savor
every little flash of fire as a separate pleasure. She slid
lower down the bed until she was lying flat on her
back, a movement that would invite him without
words.

But when she reached out to draw him close he resisted, not pulling away, but holding still, looking
down at her, soft and vulnerable beneath him. She
could see the doubt in his eyes, and sensed that his
confidence was suddenly leaving him. ''Rorke, what
is it?'' she asked urgently.

''I wish I knew what was really going on in your
head, Sara.''

''What do you mean?''

''I mean that you don't have to do this. Please believe me, you don't have to.''

She stared at him, not understanding.

''You told me once you weren't making bargains
with the jailer,'' he went on desperately. ''But how can
I know. Do you even know the truth yourself?''

Enlightenment flooded her, and with it came com-
passion for the doubts that were hurting him. She took
his face between her hands and spoke urgently.
''Rorke, it's all right. I know I don't have to fear you.''

''Tell me you're sure. Make me believe it, Sara.''

She shook her head. ''I can't *make* you believe
anything. I know I'm free to refuse you, but the only
way I can prove it is by sending you away. I won't do

that because I couldn't bear to. Haven't I already proved that once tonight?"

"But—"

"Rorke, don't torment yourself with doubts that don't make sense. Do you know so little about women that you can't tell how much I want you?"

"I know nothing at all about women like you. I've never met one before."

"Then it's about time you found out," she whispered against his mouth.

She wondered how he could possibly still have doubts after she'd welcomed him so completely. Then she remembered that Rorke knew a lot about loving, but almost nothing about being loved. She felt a surge of anger against Laurel, who'd rewarded her husband's devotion by a coldness that had left him prey to so many fears and confusions.

She could feel some of the tension flowing from him. The shoulders beneath her hands began to relax as the loving tone of her voice pierced his defenses.

Deep within him the hard knot of fear that had formed suddenly was dissolving. Her body felt good against him, but sweetest of all was the touch of her hands on his face, then on his neck as she slid them around him and exerted gentle pressure to draw him down to her. The acceptance in that gesture caused him to ache. But at the same time his strength returned in a rush, and the arms that pulled her to him were confident again.

At the back of his mind he was aware that she'd had his pride at her mercy and had returned it to him with bounteous hands. Later he'd have time to wonder about that, and about the loving wisdom that had made everything she said and did right. But now his thoughts were becoming blurred as she wrapped him around again with her magic.

He made love to her with passionate gratitude for her healing generosity. Beneath his body, her skin was warm and glowing with her response. But still he lingered, caressing her breasts with lips and hands until their taut peaks told him what he wanted to know.

To Sara, lying beneath him, the delay was an agonizing delight. She moved against him, trying to urge him onward, but now his control seemed superhuman, and he gently resisted all her efforts to take control. "Rorke—" she pleaded, almost sobbing in her frustration.

She could feel his manhood against her leg, hard with a passion that equaled her own, but he made no move to claim her. He was caressing the skin of her neck with soft kisses, just below the ear, tormenting her lovingly. The forks of passion that had once been separate sensations now came closer and closer together until they merged in one fire that roared through her. She twisted her head, writhing against him, half-demented at the friction of his hair on her soft skin.

He moved slowly across her and at once her legs parted in feverish invitation. The feel of him between her thighs was unbearably good, and in the dark warmth of that place the ache of unsatisfied desire melted as he took possession. His movements were slow and powerfully controlled, and with each one a small moan escaped her, for this was how she'd dreamed it would be between them.

Now her eagle was bearing her aloft on mighty wings. The earth was far below them as together they soared close to the sun, bathed in its golden light and fierce heat. Higher and higher he carried her, until the furnace consumed them both and she felt herself turn to molten fire. She reached out yearning hands toward the glory and discovered with wonder, that—if only for a moment—it could be hers.

Already it was passing. She was becoming herself again, a woman who was a separate being from the man she loved, and who felt that separation keenly. She longed to know if he felt the same, but in the darkness his eyes were hidden from her.

They lay together a long time, locked in each other's embrace, in the drowsy contentment of love fulfilled. She held him close, his head on her breast, feeling as though a storm had come to rest in her arms. It was he who slept first, and she was glad of it, for now she was free to whisper aloud the words that she'd been saying to him, silently, in her heart.

There's this, too, my beloved. Most of all, there's this.

Ten

Sara fought her way slowly out of sleep. It was still dark, and she couldn't have slept more than a couple of hours, but she'd been awoken by a feeling that she was looking at a jigsaw, one of whose pieces didn't fit.

She'd had this feeling once before, the night she arrived, when she'd sensed something wrong about the kitchen. She'd been right then and had learned to trust her instincts. This time she knew the answer was locked away in her mind, if only she knew where to look for it.

By her side Rorke slept soundly, one arm partly across her. She eased herself gently away from under it and slid off the bed. Her clothes still lay on the floor where Rorke had thrown them in his urgency, and beside them lay his own. She had a vague memory of helping him to strip them off, but she couldn't remember where his actions had ended and her own had

begun. She felt the cold night air on her bare skin and
before she could stop it the thought flitted across her
mind that as the weather turned colder she'd have to
start sleeping in a nightgown.

Amazed, she pulled herself up short. It was as
though she'd begun to accept that the two of them
were going to be here indefinitely. And why shouldn't
they be? she thought longingly. The rest of the world
seemed very far away. The only reality was here, in this
room, in her heart, in the singing joy of her flesh.

Through the windows she could see the landscape
silvered with moonlight, beautiful and eerie. She settled herself on a window seat, staring out raptly. She
might have been alone with him on the moon. But
soon enough the world would intrude. Someone
would realize that her phone had stayed unanswered
too long and—

That was it.

Sara sat up straight with shock as the elusive memory came to her. Fergus had said "Call me after a few
days to let me know you're all right." It had sounded
like the natural concern of a kindly man. But now she
knew that Fergus wasn't kindly, and what had seemed
innocuous before suddenly assumed a new significance.

Rorke was convinced that nobody knew where he
was, but suppose Fergus suspected and wanted to
know for certain? What better way than to let her
come here, and make her promise to call?

Her silence had lasted well over a week now, long
enough to confirm his suspicions. She couldn't work
out what he'd do next, but whatever it was Rorke was
in danger.

Sara took a step toward the bed. She'd reached out her hand to awaken him but stopped as she realized that telling Rorke would achieve nothing. To him it would just be another argument for waiting in the hope that his quarry would turn up. Sara realized that any action must be taken by her.

At that moment he turned over and Sara drew in her breath at the chance she'd suddenly been given. Rorke wore the key to the bedroom door on a chain around his neck. His movement had thrown the key onto the pillow and the clasp lay near to it. If she was careful she could free the key without touching him. Holding her breath, she reached forward.

Suddenly Rorke seized her shoulders. Sara gasped in surprise as he hauled her forward across his chest. She began to kick and struggle. She knew it was useless to fight his enormous strength, but she fought anyway to release her rage at an opportunity lost. At any other time she'd have enjoyed the sensation of his naked body wrestling hers, but now she could have wept with frustration.

For several minutes they struggled. Desperation gave her added strength and she fought back hard enough to surprise him. Even so, she could sense that he was holding back his whole power to keep from hurting her. "Sara, for God's sake, give up," he grated at last. "You know you're not going to get the better of me. I'm afraid I may hurt you."

The last word was muffled as she landed him a stinging clout on the side of the head. She heard him mutter something about being pushed too far and in another moment she was on her back, Rorke's body was on top of her frantically writhing form, and her hands were imprisoned at her sides. She glared up at him in impotent fury, aware of his thigh between her legs, the way his chest was rising and falling with his rapid breathing, and the disturbing glint in his eyes. "Don't you know better than to writhe against me like that?" he growled. "There's only one way to end this fight."

"No," she gasped, but even to her own ears her protest sounded unconvincing. She, too, had been roused by their struggle and now her skin was burning everywhere that it was in contact with his. She knew she should try to stop him, force him to listen to her, but her thoughts were growing fainter, drowned out by the roar of her senses. She made one last effort. "Rorke...please listen to me."

"No, Sara. You listen to *me*," he said against her mouth.

He'd released her wrists and ran his hands over her, tantalizing her everywhere. He knew that she, too, was at fever pitch, ready for him, and he was taking her swiftly to that place where there were no problems and their passionate antagonism could be transmuted to blazing joy.

Sara knew she should try to resist him but instead she found herself curling her fingers into his hair, then sliding them over his back, clasping him to her, telling him of her desire.

Their mating was without gentleness. He made love to her with power and vigor, and she responded in kind, meeting his passion with her own, giving him fire for fire. They were both exhausted when it was over. Rorke lay on his back, his arm beneath Sara's neck, his hand still fitted possessively around her shoulder. "Do you still want to leave me, Sara?" he asked, turning his head to look at her.

She raised herself on one elbow and looked down at him. Even now she couldn't resist running her hand over his chest, feeling the thunder of his heartbeat gradually slowing to normal beneath her palm. The sensation ravished her with delight. She wanted to return to his arms and forget the world again. But she resisted it. "I wasn't going to leave you, Rorke," she told him quietly. "Not for good, anyway. I was going to come back."

He grinned sardonically. "Sure you were. It wasn't a bad try, Sara. You're getting more ingenious, but then so am I. We agreed, didn't we, that our truce is an armed one? I won't let you escape, but I respect your right to try."

"I wasn't trying to escape, not in the sense you mean. I'm not your enemy."

He drew her close. He wasn't angry, but she knew he was as immovable in his ironic good humor as in his rage. "I know you're not," he said. "You've got this bee in your bonnet about trying to save my soul."

"I'm trying to save your life," she insisted. "Rorke, you've always been so certain that Fergus didn't know you were here, but I think he guessed and used me to find out. I've remembered things about the evening that seem strange now, the way he asked me if there was a man in my life. It sounded like small talk, but suppose he was trying to discover who was likely to search for me?

"You remember I recognized you that first night? Of course I did, because Fergus found an excuse to show me your picture. He was setting me up to meet you." She thumped the bed in her frustration. "Why wasn't I more suspicious at the time?"

"Why should you have been? You couldn't have imagined anything like this situation." He grinned. "Besides, I know your ferocious single-mindedness. All you cared about were your eagles. Fergus could have been the devil in red tights for all you'd have noticed."

"Yes, that's true. But I know it now. He really did ask me to call him from the mainland after a few days, as I told you, not because he was coming here, but because he *said* he was worried about my safety. Of course, his real reason was to confirm his suspicions about you. I'm sure he knows about your journeys down the coast to pick up supplies."

"If you're suggesting that my friend has betrayed me, that's impossible. I trust him completely."

"But someone might have seen you, not clearly but enough to make them suspicious. Fergus hasn't heard from me for a week. Maybe that's told him what he wanted to know."

He looked at her curiously. "What exactly were you going to do, Sara?"

"I was going to go to the mainland and call him, tell him a real story about how I'd been here a long time because the eagles were difficult to find, and how peaceful I'd been on my own—"

"Everything to convince him that I'm not here, huh?"

"Exactly."

"How were you going to get to the mainland?"

"I'd search until I found your boat."

"Think you could have found it before I came chasing after you?"

"Easily," she snapped. "I was going to lock you in this room."

He grinned. "Of course, I should have thought of that."

"When I'd put Fergus off your scent I was going to come back here and let you out."

He stared at her. "My God, I believe you'd have done exactly that!"

"Of course I would. I couldn't leave you here to starve to death."

"Have you any idea what kind of rage I'd have been in?"

"I think I can imagine."

"Yet you'd have come back and faced me, wouldn't you?" he asked slowly, studying her face as if he'd just seen it for the first time.

"I'd have had to."

"Sara, what do you think you'd have achieved?"

"If Fergus thought you weren't here he'd have had to abandon whatever plan he has in mind."

"And do you think that would have changed anything? Don't you know he and I have to meet sometime? For Laurel's sake I have to see him punished."

"Why?" she demanded passionately. "Didn't you do enough for her? You sacrificed your whole life to her needs. She can't demand more."

"But I can demand it *for* her. We had a kind of unspoken bargain. She'd marry me, and I'd keep her safe from Fergus. But I failed her."

"Then you're not doing this for love," she breathed, "but out of guilt."

"What does it matter why I'm doing it? I owe it to her."

"But it isn't your fault that she died. You did all you could to help her when she was alive. You can't do her any good now. Rorke, *she's dead*. You're alive, and so am I. You belong to me, not to her." She seized his hand and pressed it against one breast so that his palm was full of the soft roundness. Never taking her eyes from his face she guided his hand lower to her tiny waist, out over the flare of her hip, and down the length of one silky thigh. "Does that mean nothing to you?" she pleaded.

"You know what it means to me. You know it every time we make love."

"Then why can't we be together if we want to?"

After a long silence Rorke disengaged himself and gently pushed her away. When he spoke, his voice seemed to come from a great distance. "Because I have a promise to keep," he said quietly. "Forgive me, Sara. I should have been strong enough to stay away, but I wasn't. Perhaps I never could have been. There's nothing left of me to offer a woman. If there had been..." he hesitated and shuddered in frustration. "I wish to God I'd never met you, Sara," he said violently.

He pushed the bedclothes back with sudden force, picked up his jeans from the floor and pulled them on. Then he went to sit on the window seat, well away from her. "Go to sleep," he said harshly.

Sara was alone when she awoke the next morning, and the bedroom door stood open. She looked out into the corridor and saw the door of Rorke's room standing open, also. She dressed quickly and went in. He was standing by his window, which overlooked the front of the house. His eyes were fixed on the road that led to the shore, the road along which Fergus would have to come. He was very still and quiet.

At last he seemed to become aware of Sara and turned to look at her. "Go away, Sara," he told her. "I'll be down in a moment."

Sick at heart, she turned and left him. But her thoughts remained with that figure by the window, frightening in its stillness, waiting with terrible patience. Gradually a resolve formed in her. By the time Rorke followed her downstairs she'd made a decision that would have been incredible when she first came to Farraway a few days and so many ages ago.

At breakfast she was silent and heavy-eyed. She'd only slept briefly, and it had been restless. Before that she'd lain awake, gripped by despair, knowing that a probable tragedy was moving inexorably nearer, and that all her efforts hadn't budged Rorke one inch.

Last night he'd hinted that she'd touched his heart, but it made no difference. His promise to the dead woman came before anything he might feel for the living one. Sara had to face that fact.

Rorke, too, looked grim and there were dark smudges beneath his eyes. He'd remained on the window seat for the rest of the night, and Sara knew he hadn't slept.

He refused all food and had only coffee, which he took black and bitter. He drank it staring out of the kitchen window at the windswept moors. His broad back and the uncompromising set of his shoulders discouraged conversation, and Sara knew by instinct that he was trying to avoid looking at her. At last he set his mug down on the table and said, "I'm going out for a while."

"Rorke." She waited until he'd turned to face her before saying quietly, "You needn't lock the front door. I'm not going anywhere." She saw him look at

her wryly and added, "I'm staying here now because
you need me." He took a step toward her and stared
down into her face. His eyes were dark and puzzled,
and now that it was almost too late to matter she had
the satisfaction of knowing she'd said the one thing
that could leave him without an answer.

"Suppose I offered to let you go?" he asked at last.

She was silent a moment. "I wouldn't," she told
him at last. "I've been doing some thinking, and I
believe you're right. Fergus *is* coming here, not to look
for me, but for his own reasons. If I returned to the
mainland now I don't think I could stop him coming.
So I'm staying here."

"You still think you can talk me out of it, don't
you?"

"As long as I'm here, I can try. At any rate, whatever it is, we'll see it through together."

She kissed him. He put his arm around her and for
a moment they held each other, exchanging what
comfort they could. Then he drew away from her and
went to the front door. "Take your jacket," she said.
"There's a cold wind."

He took his jacket from a hook by the front door.
She helped him on with it and buttoned it up. He went
out, leaving the door unlocked.

Rorke almost ran the first few hundred yards. He
wanted to put as much distance as possible between
himself and Sara. He'd known as soon as he saw her
that she was trouble, but she'd turned out to be a different kind of trouble to what he'd expected. She
could rouse his hunger for her with a word, a smile or
an unconscious turn of her head. But deep as their
passion was, it wasn't at such times that she moved
him most deeply.

Today she'd moved him in a way that frightened him. She'd said "I'll stay with you," and "You need me." The words had come unexpectedly out of nowhere and hit him like a blow over the heart, reminding him of the loneliness he'd lived with for so long. Being totally alone, even while living with someone else, was something he understood and could cope with. What he couldn't cope with was Sara's warmth and generosity reaching out to him.

She'd promised that they'd see it through together, and it was like hearing the word "together" for the first time. He savored it, trying to understand it in relation to himself. With Laurel there'd been no "together". Faithful to his word, he'd cared for her and loved her to the end, but he'd always known that his love had no power to pierce the chilly barriers of the private world where she lived.

And she? Had she realized that he had needs that she might have tried to fulfill? Had she ever thought, "He needs me"? Would she have known what to do if she had?

Even at their closest moments they'd been apart, and until now he hadn't understood the true loneliness of that life.

He thought of Sara, who'd opened her arms to him despite everything he'd done. He thought of her solitary life and the way her disappearance seemed to have gone unnoticed. An inexplicable rage possessed him at the thought that no man would call him to account for the way he'd treated her. If she'd been his he'd have turned on anyone who hurt her, and he found that his hands had unconsciously clenched into fists.

In Rorke's nature, violence was curiously intermingled with an instinct to protect. He was drawn toward anyone who needed him, as Laurel once had, and as Sara now did. He wondered at the fool who'd called her hard. In her lonely defiance of him she seemed intensely vulnerable.

Then he grinned as he pictured Sara's reaction if he suggested that she needed a male protector. The thought entertained him so much that the grin turned into a crack of laughter and several seagulls who'd been swooping peacefully overhead wheeled away, scolding him noisily.

Preoccupied with his thoughts, he'd walked further than he'd noticed, and now saw that he'd almost reached the cliff. He strode the last few yards and stood there staring out over the sea. So lost in thought that it was a long time before he was aware that he was watching something moving over the water.

He flung himself to the ground and shaded his eyes with his hands, straining vainly to make out details. Now that his hopes seemed on the verge of being fulfilled, he was without his powerful binoculars. All he could make out was a boat moving in the direction of Farraway. He couldn't even see how many people were aboard.

He stayed there for several minutes while the boat drew nearer. At last he could see that it held one man, and his heart began to thud with anticipation. He eased his way back from the edge of the cliff, inch-by-inch, taking care to keep down out of the boatman's sight. Only when he'd gone back twenty feet did Rorke rise and start to run swiftly back toward the house.

Sara saw Rorke running from a distance and her heart, too, began to pound, but with fear, for she knew what it meant. She was waiting for him at the door. "Rorke, is it—"

"Someone's coming, Sara. Get inside and out of sight."

He pushed her back into the house, not roughly but brooking no refusal. When they were both inside he locked the front door and put the key in his pocket. "Upstairs," he said firmly, taking her arm.

He took her into his own bedroom, locking the door behind them. "I didn't see who it was," he said curtly, "but I'm taking no chances."

Horrified, only half believing that this was happening, Sara saw him take the shotgun from his wardrobe and check it carefully. "No," she cried passionately. "I won't let you."

She hurled herself at him, seizing the gun and wrenching it out of his hands. Rorke's face, pale and terrified, loomed close to hers, then she felt him seize her and thrust her against the wall. She heard the clatter as the gun hit the floor. Her head swam, a haze clouded her eyes, but through it she could still see the dark eyes staring with horror.

"Damn it, Sara!" he said between gritted teeth. "Do you know how dangerous what you just did was? Never do a thing like that again, do you hear me?"

He pulled her against him, crushing her tightly. She could feel him trembling and his voice shook. "Are you crazy? Do you want to get killed? If that thing had gone off...don't you know that I—Sara...*Sara*—"

She clung to him and looked up in wonder at what she'd heard in his voice. He covered her face with kisses, moving his hands possessively over her as if he was trying to reassure himself that she was still there.

At last he was still, but through his shirt she could hear his heart beating thunderously against her own.

"Don't you know," he said at last, "that you're the one person that I care about now? I can't give it up for you, Sara. Nothing can make me do that, but if you'd been hurt..." He bent his head and kissed her once more. "Don't ever try anything like that again. Promise me!"

She drew back a little and looked him in the eye. "No," she said simply. "I'll make you no promises except this one, that I'll stop you any way I can."

"Sara..."

For a moment she thought he'd explode with rage at her again, but he only turned away, a hand over his eyes. She stood watching him, seeing the pained set of his shoulders.

At last he sighed and dropped his hand. Then he grew very still. His movement away from her had brought him directly in front of the window, and now he stood transfixed, staring out at something. In a moment Sara was beside him, and her heart leapt for joy at what she saw.

The man approaching the house with steady plodding steps was Jimmy Orken.

"He must be wondering why I never sent for him," she said. "So he's come looking."

Rorke sighed. "I'm sorry, but I can't let him find you."

He moved quickly, turning her so that her back was to him. He slid one arm around her waist, drawing her against him, and put the other hand over her mouth. "Don't struggle, darling," he whispered. "It's useless."

Other struggles with Rorke had already told her how useless it was. His grip on her was almost gentle but she knew she could never break it. She stood there, imprisoned in his arms, while she tried to take in the fact that he'd called her darling.

Through the glass they could see Jimmy Orken getting closer to the house. Rorke began to back away from the window, taking her with him. "This room overlooks the front door," he said. "Luckily I locked it. Everything else is locked up. When he can't get in he'll give up and go back to the mainland."

His hand covered her mouth only lightly, and she managed to say, "Do you think he'll just leave it at that?"

"The Orkens have been in the Drummonds' employ for years. He's probably here because Fergus sent him to check up on you. With any luck he'll report back that you've inexplicably vanished, and that'll get Fergus wondering."

Remembering how Fergus had directed her to Jimmy, Sara had to admit that this sounded likely. "Rorke, *please*..." she started to say, but at once his hand tightened over her mouth.

Down below Jimmy passed from view as he approached the door. There was a brief silence, then the sound of the heavy knocker echoing through the house. Another silence, then the knocker sounded again. "Hallo!" he shouted. "Anyone at home? Miss Tancred! Hallo, there!"

Silence. Sara could only assume that Jimmy had started to walk around the house. Distantly she could hear a sound that suggested he was hammering on the kitchen door. After a while he seemed to have returned to the front.

"Hallo!" he shouted again, and the knocker thundered. As the echoes died away into silence Sara could hear the sound of Rorke's breathing very close to her ear. After a moment he began to move slowly toward the window, keeping to the side and out of sight if the man should look up.

Sara could see Jimmy now, tramping sturdily away from the house, his shoulders hunched against the wind, his form growing smaller and smaller until at last it vanished altogether.

Eleven

Sara opened her eyes to find Rorke sitting on the edge of the bed, his eyes fixed on her. Her heart gave a sickening lurch. She knew what had happened. "Is he...?"

"Yes. Fergus is on his way here. I've been keeping watch from my window since first light."

"It might be someone else, Jimmy Orken again..."

"It's Fergus. I've seen him clearly. He'll be here in a minute."

She flung back the blanket and rose swiftly, clasping her arms about him as though she could restrain him. *"No,"* she cried wildly, "think, while there's still time. It's not too late."

He held her tightly, but she knew she hadn't moved him. Desperation and panic rose in her but she fought them down. This was her last chance and it was slipping away. "Rorke, listen to me, please," she begged, pulling away and looking into his face. "If you won't think of yourself, think of me."

"Darling, it'll be all right—"

"It won't be all right. Rorke, I love you. Do you understand that?"

He shook his head. "No woman could love a man who's behaved as I have to you."

"What do you know about how a woman loves?" she cried passionately. "Did she love you? Did she give you anything that you should give her so much back? *I* love you. Don't risk everything we might have. If you kill him we'll never have anything more than that."

"I'm not going to kill him," he said quietly.

"But you might, you might," she insisted frantically. "Don't risk it, Rorke." Tears were streaming down her face. She'd never truly believed she could fail. Now the impossible was happening and she was powerless to prevent it. All her love had been useless against this moment. "Rorke, if you care for me at all . . ."

His face was pale with strain. "I do care, Sara. But I have no choice."

"Don't take the gun," she pleaded. "Anything else, but not that."

"Without the gun it'll take too long. They'll come looking for him."

"Then let me be with you when you talk to him."

"No," he said harshly. "I don't want him to see you. You're staying here."

He rose to his feet. She slid from the bed and clung to him, feeling him kiss her more tenderly than ever before. Then he gently pushed her from him, looking into her face as if for the last time. She caught one glimpse of the dreadful expression in his eyes before he pulled away from her and strode quickly to the door. It was closed before she could reach it, and the key turned in the lock.

"No!" she screamed, beating on the door. "No, Rorke please!"

But the footsteps fading on the oak floor told Sara that she'd failed. She leaned against the door, helpless tears streaming down her face, praying desperately, *Keep him safe. Let Fergus give in quickly. Don't let him turn into a murderer.*

She got dressed. As she pulled on her jeans and sweater she concentrated hard on each tiny action to take her thoughts off what might be happening below. She pulled a comb indifferently through her hair. The face that stared back from the mirror was pale and strained, the face of a woman who knew that today would decide the rest of her life, and who was full of dread at the outcome.

The silence from below was terrifying. It went on and on, a sharp-edged awareness that was like listening to a scream. Against all reason she began to hope. It was a mistake, Fergus hadn't come...

Then there was a shot!

With the sound her tears dried. She was in a desert, a barren, desolate place where there were no tears, no feelings and no pain. If there could ever be pain in this place it would be unbearable, but thankfully there was only the arid bleakness that was all she'd ever feel again.

She discovered, with faint surprise, that although dead, she could still function. Her hands seemed to move of their own accord, packing her things together. Her heart was like a stone within her. Her mind, icily efficient, waited for the sound of approaching footsteps.

At last they came, distant at first, then growing closer. There was something brutal about that heavy, purposeful tread, and she wondered how she'd never noticed it before. She drew away from the door and stood facing it, steeling herself for the ordeal of seeing Rorke's face. The footsteps halted outside, the key rattled, the door swung open.

Fergus stood there, smiling at her.

"My dear Sara," he said, "if you only knew how delighted I am to see you."

How cold his eyes were, as cold as the metal of the pistol in his hand. Pain slashed through her as she remembered the shot she'd heard. "Rorke," she whispered through dry lips.

"Still alive, my dear, for the moment. I'd have liked to finish the job straight away, so much tidier. But I had to be quite certain you were really here, otherwise how could you have killed him?"

"What are you talking about?"

"Shall we go downstairs, then I can explain to the two of you at once? It'll be simpler that way."

He stood back and indicated for Sara to come past him into the hall. As soon as she did she saw Rorke's shotgun leaning against the wall. Fergus picked it up in his free hand. "I brought it with me as a precaution," he said. "My brother-in-law was unconscious when I left him, but I daresay he's come around by now, and it seemed best not to leave this lying within his reach."

Sara began to run madly. When she reached the end of the corridor and turned the corner that led to the stairs she almost froze with dread at what she saw.

Rorke lay at the foot of the stairs, an ugly bloodstain spreading rapidly over the right shoulder of his shirt. He was frighteningly still.

Sara ran down and flung herself beside him, touching his face, crying his name beseechingly. His skin was pale and for a terrible moment she thought he was dead, but at last he opened his eyes slowly and looked straight into hers. "Sara," he whispered.

She kissed him, weeping with relief, but Fergus seized her arm from behind, yanked her to her feet and thrust her violently against the far wall. "That's enough," he snapped. "I don't want to waste time over this. It's taken too long already. Stay there!" This was addressed to Sara, who'd made a move to return to Rorke. She was forced to remain where she was, several feet away from Rorke, her gaze fixed helplessly on his agony.

Fergus stood in front of the open front door. He rested the shotgun against the wall, but kept the pistol.

"Why did you come here?" Sara demanded.

Fergus smiled. It was the pleasant smile she'd seen from him when they'd had dinner together. Now she wondered how she could have failed to see that it was full of chill menace. "I should have thought it was perfectly obvious," he said. "I daresay Rorke has told you one or two little things about me by now. I need money, a lot of it, and very badly. To be precise, I need Laurel's money. I'd have gotten it a year ago if that fool of a judge had known his job. A guilty verdict would have barred Rorke from inheriting and the money would have reverted to me at once. As it is, nothing less than his death will do."

"And you think you'll get away with it?" she burst out. "You're the first one the police will come to."

"My dear Sara, you're being absurd. When the police find two bodies here—oh, didn't I mention that you're going to die as well? How careless of me. No wonder you didn't understand.

"The police will come to inform me that two dead bodies have been found on my island. I'll identify them as my brother-in-law and a young woman who approached me for permission to come here to photograph eagles. I warned her what a lonely place this was for a solitary woman, but she wasn't worried. She told me she had a pistol. When the police find the two of you, and the two guns beside you, what do you think they'll suppose?"

"That we shot each other," Sara said in a daze. "But why should we?"

"You were trying to escape of course. Don't tell me you've been up here all this time of your own free will? After all the trouble I went to?"

"You planned it all, didn't you?" she said slowly. "You knew Rorke was here."

"Let's say I had a very strong suspicion." Fergus turned toward Rorke, who was watching him with burning eyes. "It was a good idea going so far down the coast. It might have worked if you hadn't been unlucky. One of your landings was witnessed by someone who'd moved down there from Glenrie quite recently, and who happened to owe me a favor. I offered to wipe the slate in return for a little watchfulness. It didn't take me long to work out where you were living.

"I couldn't think what you were doing here, unless it was licking your wounds. You surely weren't hoping I might have neglected to destroy Laurel's suicide note? That went up in flames before you were halfway out of the house that night."

"I knew that." Rorke's voice was harsh. "I had another idea in mind."

"So I realized when my informant told me you'd brought a shotgun across. After that it was clear that you were either planning to kill me or make my life difficult in some other way, and I knew something would have to be done soon. But I was content to leave you here until a suitable opportunity presented itself. And in the end it did. I met a woman at a party.

"Sara, dear, did you really think I was such easy game as I appeared that night? When I discovered what had fallen into my hands, I couldn't believe my luck. You're so lovely that he was bound to think I had designs on you, which would make you a useful hostage.

"I threw in the medallion he gave Laurel, just for good measure. At the very least I knew he'd be maddened at seeing it in the possession of someone he associated with me. The rest was a matter of chance. I hoped he'd keep you here as a way of luring me out into the open. If he hadn't—" Fergus shrugged "—I'd have lost nothing. But when I didn't hear from you I began to hope. I came up to have a look, but as you can see—" Fergus indicated the pistol "—I came prepared.

"Now it's just a question of arranging things artistically." He smiled dreadfully at Sara. "You fired the first shot from this pistol that will be found in your hand. But you only wounded him and he managed to discharge the shotgun at you at the same time as you fired the second shot, the one that killed him. That's what the police will assume because there'll be nothing to suggest otherwise. The two of you will be alone. I took a boat much further along the coast and I came over in poor light. Not a soul will ever know I was here.

"The bodies will be found quite naturally. No one will be surprised that you were killed by a vicious brute with one murder to his credit already."

Rorke tried to struggle to his feet, his features contorted with agony. He managed to rise to one knee but fell back against the stairs, sweat pouring down his face.

"Let her go!" he cried hoarsely. "You don't need Sara. Let her go!"

"And where would she go?" Fergus asked, coldly amused. "Running off to the police to tell them I'd killed you. Do you think I'm going to allow that to happen?"

"No one would believe her," Rorke said raggedly, "if it was obvious that I'd done it myself." He'd managed to lever himself up again. He was gasping with pain but he managed to get the words out. "You've set me up as a murderer. Everyone believes it. They wouldn't be surprised at my suicide. You'll be safe, safer than you'd ever be with two murders on your hands. They couldn't prove anything against you, no matter what Sara said. Fergus, for God's sake I'm offering you a good bargain. Let Sara go and I'll pull the trigger on myself. I'll even write you a note first but *let her go*."

"One suicide note for another, eh?" Fergus mused, grinning. "Yours in return for the one of Laurel's that I destroyed. It's a tempting offer. It appeals to my sense of natural justice. Only I doubt you could write two words with that arm now.''

"Let her go,'' Rorke begged.

Ignoring Fergus and the pistol trained on her, Sara darted forward and knelt beside Rorke, trying to support him in her arms. She could hardly speak but she managed to whisper, ''Rorke, please, it's no use. I don't want it, and he'll get away with everything. Remember your promise to her?''

He stared at her through eyes crazed with pain. ''He's going to get away with it, anyway, darling. There's nothing I can do about that. The only thing I can do now is to try to get you out of it.''

"This is all very touching,'' Fergus said wearily, ''but I really think my original plan is better. I can't help feeling that, no matter what happened, Sara would try to make trouble for me.''

"You're right,'' Sara said, looking up at him with hate-filled eyes. ''I'd go to the police and I'd *make* them believe me. You wouldn't be safe from me, Fergus. Not ever!''

"That's what I thought.'' He gripped her arm painfully, pulling her to her feet and away from Rorke. ''So you see I'm really doing the only sensible thing.'' He raised the pistol to aim it directly at Rorke.

"Sara—''

Rorke's whisper was almost inaudible, but she heard it. His eyes were on her and she saw in them everything it was too late to say, his love, his agonized plea for her forgiveness. She wrenched her arm from Fergus's grasp and ran back to Rorke, covering his body with hers. She curled her arms tightly around him and closed her eyes, waiting for the shot that would end her life.

The wait seemed to stretch for all eternity, then there was a clatter as something heavy hit the floor. She turned her head to witness the unbelievable sight of Fergus lying flat on his back while a hefty policeman looked down at him. In a corner Jimmy Orken was retrieving the pistol. "Are you all right, lassie?" asked the policeman.

"Yes, yes, never mind me," she said, bewildered.

The policeman looked at Rorke. "Is he alive?"

"Yes, but we must get him to a doctor, quickly, please."

For a moment she thought Rorke had fainted, but then he opened his eyes and looked at her. He drew her close to him with his good arm and she took him in her arms again in a moment of communion in which everything was forgotten but each other.

Jimmy had rejoined the policeman and the two of them were hauling Fergus to his feet and fixing his hands behind him in a pair of handcuffs. Fergus's face was twisted with rage, but against the combined strength of the two men he could do nothing. Jimmy thrust him none too gently onto a chair by the wall. "You can't run anywhere as you are," he said curtly, "so sit still and shut up."

"I'm Sergeant Kendry," the policeman told Sara. "Jimmy came to me because he was worried that he couldn't see any sign of you yesterday. I thought we should come back and take a look. While we were on our way here we heard a shot. So we hurried a wee bit and—" he glanced at Fergus "—heard a few things that'll take some explaining. But that's for later. The first thing is to get Mr. Calvin to the hospital. But I think we'll need a stretcher for that."

"There's some thick blankets upstairs," Sara said.

"The very thing!" the sergeant exclaimed. "Will you get one, lassie?"

They left the house a few minutes later, a strange-looking procession. First came the sergeant and Jimmy, with Rorke between them on the makeshift stretcher. Behind them came Fergus, his hands in cuffs behind him. Sara walked beside Rorke, who lay still and pale. The bloodstain on his shoulder terrified her. She fixed her eyes on the hole in his shirt, desperately trying to calculate whether the bullet had gone low enough to penetrate his lung, in which case . . .

It couldn't happen, it couldn't happen. She repeated it over and over again to herself as though chanting a spell to protect them both. They couldn't have survived so much together, only to lose each other at the last moment.

The journey down the cliff path was made with care and agonizing slowness. Even so there were some jolts that made Sara glad that Rorke appeared to have lost consciousness again. At the bottom were two boats, one of which Sara recognized as Jimmy's dinghy, and the other a powerful-looking speedboat.

"So that was yours?" the sergeant said to Fergus. "I wondered about it when we landed. You and I can use it to travel back. Mr. Calvin must go in the dinghy. There's more room and he'll have a smoother journey." He turned to Sara. "Don't fret, lassie. I'll reach the mainland well ahead of you and call for an ambulance. You'll find it waiting."

"You'll never handle something as powerful as that," Fergus sneered, jerking his head toward the speedboat. "The sensible thing would be to release my hands and let me take the controls."

"The sensible thing would be for you to try to understand that I wasn't born yesterday," the sergeant said with unruffled placidity. "Get in, Mr. Drummond. We'll sink or swim together."

He assisted Jimmy to place Rorke in the bottom of the dinghy. Sara had climbed in first and gently guided Rorke's head and shoulders to where they could rest on her lap. His breathing was shallow and had a tortured sound that tore at her heart.

She never forgot the journey to the mainland. Jimmy went slowly to make the ride smoother, but the sea was choppy and the little boat was buffeted around. Sara held Rorke's hand in hers and with every bump she felt his clasp tighten. His face had a set look that told her he was fighting not to groan.

"There it is," Jimmy said suddenly.

Sara raised her head and found that they were near enough to the mainland for her to be able to make out the ambulance on the jetty.

"We're nearly there," she whispered to Rorke. "Just hold on a little longer."

An answering clasp of his hand told her that he'd heard. She bent and kissed him softly. As she raised her head she saw that his eyes were open. They were fixed on her, dark and full of pain. There was something else there, too. Meeting his gaze Sara saw that he was bewildered. There was something he wanted to ask her, but he didn't know the words. While she waited, breathlessly hoping, his eyes slowly closed.

Twelve

"Mr. James will see you now."

"Thank you," Sara said, and walked through the door that the secretary was holding open for her.

Ian James, a large man in his fifties, rose and held out his hand for her, smiling broadly. He was the local Procurator Fiscal, which meant that he was half policeman, half public prosecutor, and since her return from the island a week ago Sara had already had one long interview with him. But this time it was she who'd insisted on a meeting.

"Sit down," he said kindly. "The coffee and biscuits are on the way in. I remembered you liked ginger biscuits."

Sara responded automatically to these courtesies. This was the man who'd prosecuted Rorke a year ago, and she knew by now that beneath his fatherly manner he was astute and could be ruthless. But today she was determined not to be deflected from her purpose.

Time had hung heavy on her hands in the last week. There'd been one trip back to the island with the sergeant to recover her things, and her interview with Ian James. Apart from this and the work involved in sending off her films to be processed, she'd had little to do. To make the hours pass she'd driven over to a nearby town and bought some fresh clothes. This morning she was wearing an elegant blue dress and jacket. It was a relief to put aside the jeans and sweaters of her working attire.

When she'd looked in the mirror that morning she'd expected to see the sophisticated Sara—the polished, successful businesswoman with her glossy mask in position. But that Sara had undergone a change and was replaced by a woman with a haunted face and anxious eyes. This woman had lived through experiences that would affect her all the days of her life. She loved a man so deeply that the rest of the world no longer existed for her, loved him so much that she'd have given her life for him. It seemed strange now to remember that once only her work had really mattered.

After the journey from Farraway, Sara had gone to the hospital with Rorke and seen him safely handed over into the hands of the doctors. He'd been taken straight into the operating room to have the bullet removed and she'd begun the long, dreadful wait. For three hours she'd paced the waiting room, wondering how she'd get through the rest of her life if Rorke should die.

At last a nurse had come to find her and, smiling, had told her that all was well. The bullet had missed the lung by a hairbreadth. "It was a delicate operation," she'd said, "but he should pull through now."

She'd been allowed to see Rorke for a moment, but he was still unconscious. Despite the multitude of tubes attached to him she'd managed to kiss him, but then she'd had to leave the intensive care unit at once. She was still haunted by the picture of him lying there pale and helpless. For that was the last time she'd seen him.

Now she came straight to the point. "Mr. James, for the last week I've been trying to get into the hospital to see Rorke, but have been told that you've given orders that I'm not to be admitted. I know he's well enough to have visitors because you've been to see him, so why am I kept out?"

"Well, the fact is, Miss Tancred, I've been rather disturbed by certain discrepancies between your statements and Mr. Calvin's. I'm sure you appreciate that he could be facing serious charges in which you may be implicated. When I realized that you were each telling a different story I'm afraid it became necessary to keep you apart."

Out of all this only three words had any impact. When Ian James spoke about facing serious charges a burning anger started deep within her and spread like a forest fire. "You don't give up, do you?" she said bitterly. "He's cleared of his wife's murder now. Fergus Drummond admitted he'd destroyed the suicide note, and both the sergeant and Jimmy overheard him. But you can't admit you were wrong about Rorke."

"But *was* I wrong about him?" Ian James asked mildly. "Between the act and the intention, where do you draw the moral line?"

"He didn't kill his wife and he never intended to kill her," Sara said emphatically.

"I accept that, but the evidence suggests that he meant to kill Fergus Drummond."

"No!" Sara said wildly. "He only—" She pulled herself up short as she saw Ian James looking at her with raised eyebrows. To say that Rorke had only meant to threaten Fergus would still put him on the wrong side of the law.

She felt as if she'd received a blow in the solar plexus. Now she realized that she should have been ready for this, but stupidly she hadn't been. Fergus was under arrest on two charges of attempted murder, one charge of assault with a deadly weapon and one of unauthorized possession of a firearm. It was so clear that the prosecutor recognized him as the villain of the piece that it hadn't occurred to Sara that he'd ask any further.

She sat staring at him, trying frantically to grapple with this fresh disaster. "Ah," Ian James said suddenly, with his beaming smile, "our refreshments have arrived."

He served Sara benignly, giving her time to gather her scattered wits. Then he chattered on, almost as if he was intent on letting her off the hook. "The guns have been analyzed for fingerprints, et cetera. There's no problem about the pistol. It had recently been fired. The bullet in Mr. Calvin's shoulder matches it, and Fergus Drummond's fingerprints are all over it.

"But there are two sets of fingerprints on the shotgun, Drummond's and Mr. Calvin's. Drummond says that when he opened the front door he found Mr. Calvin facing him on the stairs, the shotgun aimed directly at him. He says he only just stopped Mr. Calvin shooting him down in cold blood."

"Rorke had no intention of shooting him, in cold blood or any other way," Sara said emphatically.

"Well only he knows what his exact intentions were," Ian James said. "I'm more concerned with whether or not he had a gun aimed at Drummond." It might have been Sara's imagination, but his eyes contained something that was almost a warning. She chose her words with great care.

"I don't know whether he had or not," she declared with perfect truth. "I wasn't there when Drummond came in. But since Rorke was the one wounded it doesn't seem very likely that Drummond had been threatened. And two independent witnesses heard Fergus Drummond say that he'd come to Farraway with the deliberate intention of killing us both."

"Oh, without a doubt. But even a would-be murderer can tell the truth about some things. Mr. Calvin's fingerprint was on the trigger."

"Of course. He used that gun to shoot rabbits."

"Don't you think a double-barrel shotgun is a trifle excessive for rabbits?"

"He shot red deer, as well," Sara said desperately.

"It wouldn't be my choice of weapon even for red deer. Accepting that he used it for game, it still has a very premeditated look. And after the way his wife died, you must admit that he had a motive for revenge."

"I don't think it would be proper for me to speculate on Mr. Calvin's feelings," Sara said firmly.

Ian James smiled. "Have another biscuit," he said.

Sara accepted one, and a cup of coffee. She didn't want either, but it gave her time to think. "What does Rorke say about all this?" she asked at last.

"He says the gun was to threaten Drummond with," Ian James said calmly, "which, as I'm sure you realize, also carries heavy penalties."

She stared at him, feeling all hope drain away.

"However," he continued, "he admitted it when he'd only recently come around from the anesthetic, and he was still in a very drowsy state. There were no witnesses and he probably won't remember saying anything, so as a confession it's worthless."

"Yes, it is," she said, beginning to hope again.

"But he could still be charged with conspiracy."

"Conspiracy?" Sara said. "But you need two people..."

Then she saw his beatific smile and realized the trap she'd walked into.

"Exactly," he said. "You see my problem, Miss Tancred. Were you, or weren't you, on that island of your own free will? You have always maintained that you were. Mr. Calvin, on the other hand, insists that he took you prisoner and held you by force for over a week. If he's telling the truth he's committed a serious crime. If he isn't then you're implicated with him in conspiring either to murder Fergus Drummond or to threaten him with a deadly weapon. The question is, which one of you is lying to protect the other?"

There was a long silence. Then Sara lifted her head. When she spoke again it was like a gauntlet being thrown down. "Whichever one of us it is, you haven't got a case, Mr. James."

"A case for what charge?"

"Any charge at all. You can't possibly prosecute either of us without the testimony of the other. Our 'lies', if you want to put it that way, would simply cancel each other out, and you'd get laughed out of court. The best you could hope for is Not Proven, and I don't think you'll risk that, Mr. James, not after last time."

"That's a point to consider," he agreed, nodding gravely.

"You won't get either of us to damn the other," she said defiantly. "You've been bluffing to see if you can break one of us down. But it won't work."

"You might find it a little more difficult in the witness box," he suggested mildly. "A good prosecuting attorney could easily expose which of you was lying."

"I don't know that I need to be afraid of that," she said with a little shrug.

He raised an eyebrow. Out of sight Sara crossed her fingers. She was about to play her high card, and if the gamble didn't come off she had nothing left in her hand. "I don't think Scottish law allows a husband and wife to give evidence against each other," she said calmly.

"That's true," he agreed. "But are you and Mr. Calvin husband and wife?"

"Not yet, but we're going to be, just as soon as he's left the hospital."

"Unless of course I arrest one or both of you and keep you incarcerated until the trial?" He saw Sara pale and added gently, "Don't ever try to play poker, Miss Tancred. You'd give every move away in advance.

"Your clever course would have been to keep quiet about your marriage until it was too late for me to stop you. Mr. Calvin didn't mention it, although it would have been in his interests to speak out. But then, of course, I might have asked awkward questions about how long you've known each other, and how you met when he's been living on that island all this time. And there'd have been more problems because I doubt if your answers would have tallied with his. I don't suppose you'd like to tell me now, would you?''

Dumb with despair she shook her head. The prosecutor smiled again. "Good. I'm a busy man, Miss Tancred," he said. "Well, I suppose I'll have to allow you to see him now, or how will you plan the wedding? I'll give the hospital a call and tell them to let you in this afternoon.''

"Then you . . . What are you going to do?''

"If you mean am I charging Mr. Calvin with anything? No, I'm not. You can take that as final. I'm allowed to exercise a little discretion, and I don't choose to figure as the persecutor of a man who's suffered as much as Rorke Calvin has. When the truth comes out people will say that he was entitled to take the law into his own hands. In fact, if I wasn't an officer of the law . . . well, but I am.''

He got to his feet and held out a hand to her. "I think our talk's been useful on both sides, Miss Tancred," he said. "You might like to know that the final charges against Fergus Drummond will also include perjury and suppression of evidence concerning his sister's death. In addition, his arrest has led to an investigation of his business affairs and there'll probably be some charges of fraud, as well. I wouldn't be surprised if he ended up doing fifteen years.''

"So he'll pay for what he did to Laurel, after all?'' asked Sara eagerly.

"In a manner of speaking, he will. Now good day to you, Miss Tancred."

Visiting hour began at 3:00 p.m. Sara was at the hospital fifteen minutes early.

Now the moment had come, she realized that she was afraid. She loved Rorke totally. She longed to believe that he loved her, but there were so many doubts—so many thoughts that might be safer unspoken. But whatever happened, she knew she must face the shadow that lay on her heart.

She'd tried to convince the prosecutor that Rorke's wounds cleared him of suspicion, but she couldn't convince herself. Remembering the grim determination on Rorke's face as he'd left her, she had no hope that he could possibly have thrown his gun away. Fergus must have fired the first shot by chance.

The cruel truth was that she'd failed. She'd opened her arms and her heart to Rorke, offering him herself, but it hadn't been enough. She recalled his desperate offer to sacrifice his life for her—surely that meant he loved her? But it wasn't that simple. He'd believed he was going to die at Fergus's hands, anyway, and he'd had nothing to lose.

She loved him. She was his if he wanted her. But the bitter knowledge would always lie between them. She'd fought Laurel for his heart, and all their lives she'd feel that Laurel had won.

At three o'clock a nurse led her along the corridor to Rorke's small room and left her at the door. Sara hesitated, then entered.

He was lying propped up on pillows, his gaze fixed on the door. As soon as she saw him Sara knew that he'd been waiting for her. There was a look of anx-

ious intensity on his face that relaxed the moment she
appeared. He reached his good arm out to her, but for
a moment she couldn't move. She stood there, her
heart in her eyes, shaking with the violence of her
emotion. Then she ran across the room and into his
embrace. But she drew back. "I'm afraid to touch
you," she said huskily.

"I'm all right on this side. Put your arms around
me, darling. *Kiss me.*"

She raised her face and felt his lips on hers for the
first time in so many unhappy days. Joy flooded her
at the achingly sweet, familiar feeling. She drew her
arms possessively around his neck and gently held him
closer.

"I've thought about nothing else all week," he
murmured against her mouth. "I've been hazy with
sedatives half the time, but you were always there in
my heart, kissing me."

"I wanted to stay with you, but they wouldn't allow me in the room," she whispered. "But now I'm
here I'll never leave you again, my darling."

For a long time they were silent, locked in each
other's arms. Pressed against him, she could tell how
much thinner he was. The arm that held her was still
strong, but when she looked at his face again it was
pale and his cheeks were hollowed. "You look tired,
Rorke," she said, drawing back slightly to see him
better.

"I'm all right. The strain of not seeing you was unbearable. I kept thinking that you'd be here the next
time I opened my eyes, but you never were. I thought
you'd gone away and left me because you couldn't
forgive me for what I'd done. You nearly died be-

cause I was a stupid, blind, stubborn fool. How could you ever forgive that?''

For an answer she kissed him again. "You should have known I'd never leave you," she told him. "I was here the first day, during the operation. I was terrified that you might die. When it was over they let me come in for a moment, but Ian James put a ban on my visiting.''

"I know. I eventually found that out. When I heard that you were denying that I'd kept you there by force I nearly went crazy. Sara, don't you realize how bad it could have looked for you?''

"I didn't until this morning. I went to see Ian James and he as good as threatened me with a conspiracy charge if I didn't say you kidnapped me.''

"Yes, he told me.''

"Told you? When?''

"He called me as soon as you left. He said there'd be no charges against me, and so he'd lifted the ban.''

She felt a nervous blush begin to spread over her cheeks. "Did he say anything else?'' she asked.

"Yes, he said not to forget to invite him to the wedding. He added that I'm a very lucky man.''

The blush grew fiery. "Forget that foolishness,'' she told him hastily. "I was trying to frighten him out of pressing charges against you by making him think he couldn't force us to give evidence against each other. He'd backed me into a corner and I took a gamble, but I guess it didn't work.'' She sighed. "I've never been terribly good at strategic planning or outguessing an opponent.''

"I know,'' he said gently. "You're the most totally impulsive, uncalculating person I've ever known.

That's what I..." He checked himself. "Well, anyway..."

"Rorke, I only said it to stop him from pressing charges, but he isn't going to anyway, so let's forget it." She hurried the words out, gruff with embarrassment.

"You're right," he agreed. "I couldn't let you marry me for such a reason, and I'd never ask for such a reason, so we'll forget it."

"Yes," she echoed firmly, to cover the ache in her heart.

"Mr. James sent you a message. Would you like to hear it?"

"Yes, please," she muttered.

"He asked me to apologize to you about this morning. He said it was necessary, but he wasn't sure you understood why."

"Necessary?" she echoed indignantly. "To put me through all that?"

"Stop and think a moment. We told different stories, which made things awkward. He's an officer of the law. He couldn't come right out and tell us to get our act together, so he gave you a demonstration of what would happen if we didn't, and left you to work out the implications. He's a wise man, and a very kind one."

"Kind? He's the man who tried to put you away for murder."

"With the evidence Fergus gave him, he had to prosecute. But, within his official limits, he was decent to me, and I always sensed that he personally thought me innocent. When he told me this morning that he was reopening the case and my name was bound to be cleared, he sounded very pleased."

"Cleared," she echoed, savoring the word with joy. "And Fergus will go to jail for a long time, so you've got everything you wanted."

"Not everything," he said quietly. "I still don't have you."

"But—"

"I said I wouldn't marry you to save myself, and I won't. You gave me back my life. I wouldn't ask a sacrifice of you, as well."

"It wouldn't be a sacrifice," she said urgently. "What do you think I—"

"Hush, darling, let me speak. There's something I have to say to you first. After you've heard it, you decide what's to happen to us—"

"Rorke, please," she interrupted quickly. "There are some things we shouldn't talk about."

"But I have to tell you this. There was a time when I wondered if I was going to die, and the worst thing of all was the thought that then you'd never know the truth. You have to listen, and you must believe me, however difficult it is. Sara, I did it your way. At least, I was going to, if I'd had the chance."

She stared at him, wild with hope. "What do you mean?"

"I unlocked the front door, and then went to stand on the bottom stair, directly facing the door. I raised the shotgun in readiness, and when the door opened Fergus came straight into my sights.

"And then something happened to me. It was as though I'd been looking through a dark glass and suddenly it splintered and I saw things that had always been there, but my own hate and bitterness had obscured them.

"I saw that you'd been right. I hated him so much that I wasn't safe with that gun in my hand. It would have been terrifyingly easy to kill him, and then I'd have cut myself off from you. We'd never be together, and we have to be. I didn't know until that moment what you'd come to mean to me—life and warmth and love—all the things I'd forgotten existed. I couldn't risk losing them. I knew I had to come back to your world, and beg you to let me live in it with you.

"So I lowered the gun, mistakenly giving Fergus a clear shot. Sara, darling, don't cry!"

He held her close while her shoulders shook with the storm. She was weeping with relief and happiness as despair passed away. For the first time there was no shadow on her love. For her, too, the darkness had lifted and the world was bathed in sunlight. In that warm, healing light they could live together.

When she'd calmed, Rorke continued, "I don't mean that I'd given up the idea of making Fergus pay for what he'd done. If he hadn't shot me I was going to force him to talk however I could. As it is, he's gotten what he deserved in another way."

"You gave her justice in the end," Sara said slowly. She pulled back and looked into his face. "Rorke, is Laurel still there?"

He didn't have to ask what she meant. He shook his head somberly. "I loved her when she needed me, but she doesn't need me now. Never fear any ghosts, Sara. I'm free."

"Free," she echoed disbelievingly.

"I've wanted to tell you all this, but at the same time I was afraid to. It matters so much that you should love me, but I can't see any reason why you should.

You brought me back to life. Now you must tell me whether I have anything to live for."

"Love you?" she echoed. "Don't you know that I love you? I told you I did."

"Yes, on the morning Fergus arrived, when you were desperate to stop me," Rorke remembered. "I told myself then that you couldn't mean it, that you'd have said anything to hold me back.

"But then," he went on hesitantly, "you threw yourself between me and Fergus's gun, and I didn't know what to think. And today, Ian James told me that you wouldn't testify against me, no matter what threats he made. So I began to hope. But how can I believe it? I've never given you any reason to love me."

"Except that you need loving very badly," she said. "I can't think of a better reason than that."

It was true. He wouldn't be an easy man to love. He was scarred and battered, and some of his demons would always haunt him. But he needed her from the depths of his stark, uncompromising nature. Even the eagle will come tamely to the hand it loves.

"Can you put up with me?" Rorke asked insistently. "I'm no bargain as a husband. I'll be difficult to live with and you'll probably always earn more than I do. You see," he hesitated, "although I've inherited Laurel's money..."

"You don't want to use it, do you?" she said.

"Not for us to live on, no. I thought of letting it accumulate and using it to make some provision for our children later. But I don't think I could spend it myself. Do you mind very much?"

"Of course not. I think you're right."

"I'll have my writing, but I should warn you that philosophy never was a lucrative subject. On the other hand I can write anywhere, so I'll be able to come with you when you travel."

"You think I might need protecting?" she asked, trying to kiss the frown from his forehead.

He grinned suddenly. "Of course. You don't know when you're going to meet up with a savage chicken."

She laughed with him, but almost at once the laughter faded from his face. For a moment the shadow was there again as he thought of what he might have thrown away. She understood and reached up to take his face in her hands.

"Thank you," she said softly, "for coming back to me."

He took hold of her hand, noticing how it was almost swallowed up in his great fist, and thinking how perfectly they fitted together to make a whole. That was the life she'd given him, only complete when she was there.

She gave herself up to his embrace, trying to communicate the wordless message of her heart as she'd done many times before. But this time was different. Now he was ready for what she had to give. There were years ahead of them, filled with laughter and warmth and love, swift-flowing passion and slow, deep affection. There'd be sun and wine and the sweet feel of his child in his arms, all the good things of life that he'd almost lost, but which she'd given back to him.

*   *   *   *   *

*...and now an exciting short story
from Silhouette Books.*

*

HEATHER GRAHAM POZZESSERE

Shadows on the Nile

CHAPTER ONE

Alex could tell that the woman was very nervous. Her fingers were wound tightly about the arm rests, and she had been staring straight ahead since the flight began. Who was she? Why was she flying alone? Why to Egypt? She was a small woman, fine-boned, with classical features and porcelain skin. Her hair was golden blond, and she had blue-gray eyes that were slightly tilted at the corners, giving her a sensual and exotic appeal.

And she smelled divine. He had been sitting there, glancing through the flight magazine, and her scent had reached him, filling him like something rushing through his bloodstream, and before he had looked at her he had known that she would be beautiful.

John was frowning at him. His gaze clearly said that this was not the time for Alex to become interested in a woman. Alex lowered his head, grinning. Nuts to John. He was the one who had made the reservations so late that there was already another passenger between them in their row. Alex couldn't have remained silent anyway; he was certain that he could ease the flight for her. Besides, he had to know her name, had to see if her eyes would turn silver when she smiled. Even though he should, he couldn't ignore her.

"Alex," John said warningly.

Maybe John was wrong, Alex thought. Maybe this was precisely the right time for him to get involved. A woman would be the perfect shield, in case anyone was interested in his business in Cairo.

The two men should have been sitting next to each other, Jillian decided. She didn't know why she had wound up sandwiched between the two of them, but she couldn't do a thing about it. Frankly, she was far too nervous to do much of anything.

"It's really not so bad," a voice said sympathetically. It came from her right. It was the younger of the two men, the one next to the window. "How about a drink? That might help."

Jillian took a deep, steadying breath, then managed to answer. "Yes...please. Thank you."

His fingers curled over hers. Long, very strong fingers, nicely tanned. She had noticed him when she had taken her seat—he was difficult not to notice. There was an arresting quality about him. He had a certain look: high-powered, confident, self-reliant. He was medium tall and medium built, with shoulders that nicely filled out his suit jacket, dark brown eyes, and sandy hair that seemed to defy any effort at combing it. And he had a wonderful voice, deep and compelling. It broke through her fear and actually soothed her. Or perhaps it was the warmth of his hand over hers that did it.

"Your first trip to Egypt?" he asked. She managed a brief nod, but was saved from having to comment when the stewardess came by. Her companion ordered her a white wine, then began to converse with her quite normally, as if unaware that her fear of flying had nearly rendered her speechless. He asked her what she did for a living, and she heard herself tell him that she was a music teacher at a junior college. He responded easily to everything she said, his voice warm and concerned each time he asked another question. She didn't think; she simply answered him, because flying had become easier the moment he touched her. She even told him that she was a widow, that her husband had been killed in a car accident four years ago, and that she was here now to fulfill a long-held dream, because she had always longed to see the pyramids, the Nile and all the ancient wonders Egypt held.

She had loved her husband, Alex thought, watching as pain briefly darkened her eyes. Her voice held a thread of sadness when she mentioned her husband's name. Out of nowhere, he wondered how it would feel to be loved by such a woman.

Alex noticed that even John was listening, commenting on things now and then. How interesting, Alex thought, looking across at his friend and associate.

The stewardess came with the wine. Alex took it for her, chatting casually with the woman as he paid. Charmer, Jillian thought ruefully. She flushed, realizing that it was his charm that had led her to tell him so much about her life.

Her fingers trembled when she took the wineglass. "I'm sorry," she murmured. "I don't really like to fly."

Alex—he had introduced himself as Alex, but without telling her his last name—laughed and said that was the understatement of the year. He pointed out the window to the clear blue sky—an omen of good things to come, he said—then assured her that the airline had an excellent safety record. His friend, the older man with the haggard, world-weary face, eventually introduced himself as John. He joked and tried to reassure her, too, and eventually their efforts paid off. Once she felt a little calmer, she offered to move, so they could converse without her in the way.

Alex tightened his fingers around hers, and she felt the startling warmth in his eyes. His gaze was appreciative and sensual, without being insulting. She felt a rush of sweet heat swirl within her, and she realized with surprise that it was excitement, that she was enjoying his company the way a woman enjoyed the company of a man who attracted her. She had thought she would never feel that way again.

"I wouldn't move for all the gold in ancient Egypt," he said with a grin, "and I doubt that John would, either." He touched her cheek. "I might lose track of you, and I don't even know your name."

"Jillian," she said, meeting his eyes. "Jillian Jacoby."

He repeated her name softly, as if to commit it to memory, then went on to talk about Cairo, the pyramids at Giza, the Valley of the Kings, and the beauty of the nights when the sun set over the desert in a riot of blazing red.

And then the plane was landing. To her amazement, the flight had ended. Once she was on solid ground again, Jillian realized that Alex knew all sorts of things about her, while she didn't know a thing about him or John—not even their full names.

They went through customs together. Jillian was immediately fascinated, in love with the colorful atmosphere of Cairo, and not at all dismayed by the waiting and the bureaucracy. When they finally reached the street she fell head over heels in love with the exotic land. The heat shimmered in the air, and taxi drivers in long burnooses lined up for fares. She could hear the soft singsong of their language, and she was thrilled to realize that the dream she had harbored for so long was finally coming true.

She didn't realize that two men had followed them from the airport to the street. Alex, however, did. He saw the men behind him, and his jaw tightened as he nodded to John to stay put and hurried after Jillian.

"Where are you staying?" he asked her.

"The Hilton," she told him, pleased at his interest. Maybe her dream was going to turn out to have some unexpected aspects.

He whistled for a taxi. Then, as the driver opened the door, Jillian looked up to find Alex staring at her. She felt…something. A fleeting magic raced along her spine, as if she knew what he was about to do. Knew, and should have protested, but couldn't.

Alex slipped his arm around her. One hand fell to her waist, the other cupped her nape, and he kissed her. His mouth was hot, his touch firm, persuasive. She was filled with heat; she trembled…and then she broke away at last, staring at him, the look in her eyes more eloquent than any words. Confused, she turned away and stepped into the taxi. As soon as she was seated she turned to stare after him, but he was already gone, a part of the crowd.

She touched her lips as the taxi sped toward the heart of the city. She shouldn't have allowed the kiss; she barely knew him. But she couldn't forget him.

She was still thinking about him when she reached the Hilton. She checked in quickly, but she was too late to acquire a guide for the day. The manager suggested that she stop by the Kahil bazaar, not far from the hotel. She dropped her bags in her room, then took another taxi to the bazaar. Once again she was enchanted. She loved everything: the noise, the people, the donkey carts that blocked the narrow streets, the shops with their beaded entryways and beautiful wares in silver and stone, copper and brass. Old men smoking water pipes sat on mats drinking tea, while younger men shouted out their wares from stalls and doorways. Jillian began walking slowly, trying to take it all in. She was occasionally jostled, but she kept her hand on her purse and sidestepped quickly. She was just congratulating herself on her competence when she was suddenly dragged into an alley by two Arabs swaddled in burnooses.

"What—" she gasped, but then her voice suddenly fled. The alley was empty and shadowed, and night was coming. One man had a scar on his cheek, and held a long, curved knife; the other carried a switchblade.

"Where is it?" the first demanded.

"Where is what?" she asked frantically.

The one with the scar compressed his lips grimly. He set his knife against her cheek, then stroked the flat side down to her throat. She could feel the deadly coolness of the steel blade.

"Where is it? Tell me now!"

Her knees were trembling, and she tried to find the breath to speak. Suddenly she noticed a shadow emerging from the darkness behind her attackers. She gasped, stunned, as the man drew nearer. It was Alex.

Alex...silent, stealthy, his features taut and grim. Her heart seemed to stop. Had he come to her rescue? Or was he allied with her attackers, there to threaten, even destroy, her?

* * * * *

Watch for Chapter Two of SHADOWS ON THE NILE coming next month—only in Silhouette Intimate Moments.

Silhouette Desire

COMING NEXT MONTH

#385 LADY BE GOOD—Jennifer Greene
To Clay, Liz was a lady in the true sense of the word, but she wanted more from him than adoration from afar—she wanted him to be this particular lady's man.

#386 PURE CHEMISTRY—Naomi Horton
Chemist Jill Benedict had no intention of ever seeing newsman Hunter Kincaid again. Hunter was bent on tracking her down and convincing her that they were an explosive combination.

#387 IN YOUR WILDEST DREAMS—Mary Alice Kirk
Caroline Forrester met Greg Lawton over an argument about a high school sex ed course. It didn't take long for them to learn that they had a thing or two to teach each other—about love!

#388 DOUBLE SOLITAIRE—Sara Chance
One look at Leigh Mason told Joshua Dancer that she was the woman for him. She might have been stubbornly nursing a broken heart, but Josh knew he'd win her love—hands down.

#389 A PRINCE OF A GUY—Kathleen Korbel
Down-to-earth Casey Phillips was a dead ringer for Princess Cassandra of Moritania. Dashing Prince Eric von Lieberhaven convinced her to impersonate the kidnapped heiress to the throne, but could she convince him he was her king of hearts?

#390 FALCON'S FLIGHT—Joan Hohl
Both Leslie Fairfield and Flint Falcon were gamblers at heart—but together they found that the stakes were higher than either had expected when the payoff was love. Featuring characters you've met in Joan Hohl's acclaimed trilogy for Desire.

AVAILABLE NOW